BURNED

BURNED

TITANIUM SECURITY SERIES

By Kaylea Cross

Copyright © 2013 by Kaylea Cross

★ ★ ★ ★ ★

Cover Art by LFD Designs For Authors

★ ★ ★ ★ ★

This book is a work of fiction. The names, characters, places, and incidents are products of the writer's imagination or have been used fictitiously and are not to be construed as real. Any resemblance to persons, living or dead, actual events, locales or organizations is entirely coincidental.

All rights reserved. With the exception of quotes used in reviews, this book may not be reproduced or used in whole or in part by any means existing without written permission from the author.

ISBN: 978-1494734220
Print Edition

Dedication

I dedicate this book to my long-suffering husband, Todd, whose sense of fun and humor balances out my more serious nature. Thanks for putting up with me, hon! The Van Halen references in this one should make you smile. xo

Author's Note

This is the third book of my Titanium Security series, and I hope you enjoy Sean and Zahra's story. I love how Sean's fun-loving personality brings some light into Zahra's dark world, and that he's strong enough to win her trust.

Up next…Ex Marine Scout/Sniper Blake Ellis and the woman he shouldn't want but can't stop thinking about.

Happy reading!
Kaylea Cross

CHAPTER ONE

Malik Hassani ordered his bodyguards and the two other men from the room before making the call. Once the door shut behind the last man, he crossed the carpeted floor of the office in the house where he'd taken up residence and sank into the plush leather chair behind the wide mahogany desk. His men were trustworthy to a point, but he hadn't become a senior official in the Inter-Services Intelligence by being naive. That's why he'd personally swept the room for bugs when he'd entered it this morning, alone.

Once he was ready to begin, he took an encrypted phone from the intricate wood inlaid center drawer and paused another moment to collect himself before dialing the number he'd memorized more than a week ago.

It was very late on the US East coast but he didn't worry that the person he was calling might not answer. Not with the leverage he had over them.

"Hello?" the contact answered on the third ring, the voice low and fearful. With good reason. They both knew Malik was the only other person who had the number.

He didn't waste time on pleasantries because he wasn't in a pleasant mood. "I assume you know what happened yesterday?"

A pause, followed by a hard sigh. "Yes."

"The operation was a complete failure," he snapped, his temper surging. "My operative is dead and all of the targets are still alive. This is unacceptable." He was infuriated that the American security team had thwarted his plans twice now. Worse, they had signed on for contract work with the NSA and now Malik had been forced to take added protective measures, using various hideouts and relying on the loyalty of his men to keep him from being captured or killed. He'd planned far too carefully for the opportunity to eventually seize control of the Pakistani political machine and he wasn't about to jeopardize that now.

He wasn't stupid enough to trust his men's loyalty any more than necessary. Money in the amount the Americans were throwing around to garner information about him could prove a powerful and irresistible lure. At this point his best advantage was that the global intelligence agencies thought he was across the border somewhere in Afghanistan, when in reality he hadn't left Pakistan. But that element of surprise wouldn't last much longer with the amount of international pressure to find him.

He drew in a calming breath. "I want this taken care of now. Not tomorrow, not next week. *Now.*" The Titanium security team members had exposed him in the first place. He wanted them all eliminated for that, and killing them on American soil would make it clear he had the means to get to anyone he wanted, whenever and *wherever* he wanted. The way Mohammed—an operative his advisors had tapped as the most capable for the previous job—had botched the hit on the NSA safe house was an embarrassment he planned to erase with this next act.

"I gave you the information you needed," the contact shot back, clearly pushed to the limit. "I've done everything you've demanded of me, at huge personal risk, and it's not my fault your operative didn't do what he was supposed to."

"We both know you face a much greater risk than losing your job or going to jail," he retorted coldly. The photos he'd sent of the children at their private school in Jordan had made it clear his was no idle threat.

A brittle silence filled the line and Malik heard a hard swallow. "Don't…don't hurt them. You promised me you wouldn't hurt them if I did everything you said and I have—"

"I promised not to hurt them if you complied with what I need done, and what I need done has definitely *not* been accomplished yet. Do you understand that?"

"Y-yes."

No tears, and thank Allah. There were few things more irritating than having to listen to someone weeping. That sort of shameful weakness sickened Malik. "I have someone else in place in Baltimore," he continued, consciously softening his tone. "All I need is the team's new location and he'll take care of the rest."

"But I don't know where they are anymore—no one does. Because of the bombing the team's being split up and everyone's moving to new secret locations that only they and the Director know about. There's no way I can find their locations without them knowing it's me."

The pleading edge to the tone grated on Malik's nerves. "Then you had best find a way, hadn't you? Innocent lives are depending on it."

That implicit threat did its job. The answer he wanted came a moment later. "I'll find them. I'll find the locations, okay? Just swear you'll give me some time and you won't do anything to—" Another swallow, and a clearing of the throat, as though saying the names aloud would make the idea of losing them too real. "Please. They mean everything to me."

"I know they do." They were the reason he'd been able to solicit the mole's cooperation in the first place. And since then he'd received new, even more enticing information about a member of the NSA-sanctioned team that he intended to put to use shortly. But first… "I need those locations, fast. Get them to me within a few days or I'll impose a deadline you won't want to be up against."

"All right, I understand," the contact said hurriedly. "It's going to take me some time. I'm not even sure how to go about doing this."

"You'll find a way." The family's lives depended on it.

Without waiting for a response he hung up and placed the phone on his desk as he called his men back into the room. He'd dispose of the phone himself later when he was sure no one was around to see. His bodyguards entered first, both former Special Ops from the Pakistani military, followed by two of his most trusted men who had both served under him in the ISI. He had many supporters within the military and intelligence community. Powerful men who shared his vision for a new Pakistan and abhorred the weakness of the current government that made the country an American ally. And those same men would help him seize control when the right moment came.

"The contact is going to find us the new locations," Malik announced in Urdu. "In the meantime, call Amir and give him his first instructions when he's at the designated place. This new information could be the opportunity we need to start eliminating our enemies." He tapped the closed file on the desktop. "I want to send a message to the world that this is only the beginning of the attacks to come in America."

"Just Amir alone? You don't want us to have backup ready?" one of his men asked in confusion.

"Not until we have the exact locations. I'll determine the next course of action then. Understood?"

"Yes, sir," the two men answered.

Malik waved a dismissive hand at them. "Go."

One of the men opened his mouth to argue but thought better of it and pivoted to leave. Malik looked over at his bodyguards, both positioned by the door. "You as well."

They cast each other a silent look, then turned and walked out.

When the door shut behind them and he was alone once again, Malik eased back into his chair and opened the manila file folder on his desk. If the team locations didn't pan out, this information was likely to prove very useful. But even if the mole didn't find the locations, he had no compunction whatsoever about carrying out the threat he'd made. He'd expose the mole and kill the family to ensure that no one would ever dare cross him.

He closed the file and picked up the phone to destroy it and erase any evidence of the call.

Pakistan required a strong leader who understood the country's true place on the global scale, and was unafraid of wielding the ruthless hand necessary to make their homeland an Islamic nuclear superpower. Malik was that man, and he'd earned his reputation for ruthlessness for good reason.

As Zahra Gill and her teammates were about to discover firsthand.

Zahra shoved the last of the cutlery from the kitchen drawer into the cardboard packing box and reached for the canister of cooking utensils placed next to the stove. She'd moved enough to know to leave the bathroom and kitchen for last. But then, she'd never had to pack this fast before.

Her heart drummed an erratic tattoo against her ribs. It was almost five, just three hours since her boss had called to give her the news. Some of the Titanium guys would be here any minute to do the heavy lifting and she still had a thousand little things to do.

After wrapping up the dishes and glasses in newspaper in the hopes that they'd survive the trip to her new place, she raced to her bedroom to pack away the items in her bathroom. Even with the air conditioning on she was sweating in the late September warmth. She swiped the back of her hand across her damp forehead and hastily dumped all her toiletries into a small duffle she'd left on the tile floor, refusing to let herself get emotional. Since the bombing at the NSA's so-called safe house two days ago, she'd had enough to worry about without this added stress. Didn't matter that she'd lived in this place for almost two years and loved her two bedroom apartment. So what? It was just a place she'd rented. Stupid to feel so emotional over it. Like she was being torn away from a security blanket or something.

Her life was way more valuable than her attachment to this stupid apartment.

Lugging the duffle into her bedroom, she dropped it next to her already stripped double bed. She took a deep breath before forcing herself to deal with the remaining items she'd purposely left for last. On the night table with her reading lamp sat a framed picture of her and her mother. Beside it lay her mother's most cherished possession, a gold filigreed broach inlaid with a tiny ring of sapphires around the edge.

Zahra took the frame and carefully wrapped it up in one of her thickest sweaters before placing it on top of the clothes packed into the large suitcase resting on the bare mattress. Turning back for the broach, she exhaled then curled her fingers around it. The piece was beautiful, a family heirloom presented to her mother on her wedding day.

Swallowing, Zahra closed her fist around the cool surface and tucked it away deep into the pile of clothes. "I'll be okay, Mom. Don't worry," she murmured, and zipped the suitcase closed with difficulty. It was gonna be heavy, at least seventy pounds. Because of her bad hip, for a moment she thought about waiting for one of the guys to help, but dismissed it. All she had to do was get it on the floor.

She gripped the handle with both hands and tugged, setting one knee against the edge of the mattress to lug it backward. It slid fine until it reached the fulcrum point at the edge. Bracing herself, she tensed her muscles and gingerly eased it forward a few more inches. The suitcase tipped over and started its inevitable fall. Normally she'd let it hit the floor and not care but with the framed photo in there she tried to slow the descent.

The inevitable happened. Her right hip locked and every muscle in the vicinity grabbed in protest.

A sharp cry of pain escaped as she froze and grabbed for the mattress to keep from toppling to the floor. The suitcase slammed into the ground, just missing her feet. Eyes closed, trying to breathe through the agony shooting through her damaged joint, she stayed very still until the worst of the spasms had stopped. Almost afraid to move, knowing she'd suffer for days because she'd been too stubborn to let someone else move the freaking suitcase, she straightened slowly. Then hissed through her teeth when another fiery bolt shot through her hip, like someone had plunged a red-hot knife into her.

Dammit, now she wouldn't be able to walk without her cane and everyone would see her. Pressing her lips together, she wiped a hand over her damp face and took stock. The hated reminder of her injury was in her closet, hidden from view. She hadn't used it in almost a year, not since her sadistic physiotherapist had been particularly mean or she'd overdone it early on in her rehab.

Cursing her stubbornness, she hopped and hobbled her way to the closet and grabbed the damn thing. She'd just leaned on it to take her first step back to the bed when her cell rang in her back pocket. Expecting it to be Alex, her boss, she was surprised to see an unfamiliar number and hesitated only a moment before answering.

"It's Hunter," the deep male voice said. "We're downstairs and everything's clear. You ready for us?"

Yeah, I can't wait for you all to see me hobbling around like an eighty year old with a hip replacement. But the urgency of the situation far outweighed her discomfort and self-consciousness. "Sure, come on up."

"See you in a minute." He hung up before she could say anything else.

Zahra headed out of her bedroom and toward the front door, grimacing at the shocks of pain zinging through her right hip, buttock and thigh with every step. There was no way she could fake being able to move without the cane. Resigned, she steadied herself against the door jamb and waited for the sound of footsteps outside in the hallway. A moment later, through the peephole she saw them coming. She stood back to open the chain and deadbolt, then swung the door wide open.

Hunter Phillips, team leader of the Titanium Security group working with the NSA-sanctioned taskforce, nodded at her and stepped inside. He was a big, intimidating ex-SEAL with harsh features and an all-business attitude that made him seem unapproachable at first. He ran a hand over his short, dark brown hair, his honey-brown gaze taking in the bare state of her apartment with a single, assessing glance. "All packed, or do you need a hand?"

"No, everything's pretty much done. Where do you want to start?"

"Bedroom, I think." He looked past her out into the hallway and jerked his head in the direction of her room. "Let's get the mattress out first," he said to whoever stood outside.

Zahra turned her head to see who he was talking to and her heart gave a funny little flutter when Sean Dunphy strode in. She drank in the sight of his angular, olive toned-face and those dark, espresso eyes that missed nothing. His jet black hair was a little longer than she normally liked on a guy, styled into tousled peaks in front and falling to his collar in back, but it looked so soft her fingers itched to run through it. Dressed in faded jeans and a gray Van Halen T-shirt that hugged his muscular chest and shoulders and molded to his flat belly, she couldn't deny that the man stirred something inside her on a primitive level.

No, she told herself sternly. *No men, just cats for at least the next six months. You swore it in front of Claire.* Not that her fellow NSA analyst co-worker had believed her.

But it was so, so hard to remember the vow with this man standing right in front of her.

The former FORECON Marine flashed her a smile that made his bottomless brown eyes twinkle. A slightly flirtatious gleam mixed with the mischievous glint she was so used to seeing there. "Ready to go?"

As ready as she'd ever be. "Yeah. Thanks for helping."

He waved her thanks away. "No problem." She propped the door wide open behind him as he followed Hunter into her room. Without being able to help them now she made her way over to the kitchen table and gingerly eased into one of the chairs, biting her lip to hold back a curse when the muscles seized again. More sweat dotted her brow and upper lip. She wiped it away and waited for the men to emerge.

They came out a minute later carrying her mattress. Sean raised his eyebrows at her as he approached, holding the back end of it. "Sitting down on the job while we do all the hard work, huh?"

She put on a smile, embarrassed and dreading the moment when he realized she was hurt. "Just taking a bit of a rest."

He ran his gaze over her and she saw the exact instant when he noticed the cane she'd tried to hide beneath the table on the chair next to her. He stopped walking and his eyes flashed back up to hers, a frown marring his brow. Hunter stopped too and looked over at her curiously as Sean asked, "You okay?"

"Fine. Just tweaked my hip and I can't get around very easily right now, that's all."

He looked like he wanted to say more but Hunter tugged on the other end of the mattress and pulled him forward. "Sit tight then and let us handle everything, okay?"

"Okay. Sorry about this." She felt stupid just sitting there while they did all the work.

"Don't be. We'll be back up in a few minutes."

She nodded, frustrated that she had no choice in the matter anyhow.

They carried the mattress through the open door and left her alone, and she was grateful. With their extensive military backgrounds in Tier-one units and superhuman observational skills, both men noticed things others didn't. And Zahra didn't plan on talking about her past with either of them.

Not quite two hours later Sean was covered in sweat and his muscles burned pleasantly from carting all of Zahra's furniture down the narrow staircase of the apartment building. The third member of their team helping out with the move, a former Marine Scout/Sniper named Blake Ellis, pushed the solid walnut dresser back against the side of the U-Haul with a grunt and turned to face him and Hunter as he dusted his hands off.

"That all the big stuff?" he asked.

"Think so," Hunter answered. "Just clothes and a few more boxes left after we take care of the kitchen table and chairs."

"Next time you get to be the hired help and *I'll* take lookout," Sean told Ellis dryly.

The guy's smile flashed white against his darker skin. "We'll see."

Sean snorted and headed back upstairs with Hunter only to find Zahra trying to roll a suitcase toward the door while balancing awkwardly on her cane, her long black ponytail swinging against her shoulder blades. From the beads of sweat he could see on her brow, Sean knew she was in a lot more pain than she'd let on.

"Whoa, what are you doing? I told you we'd handle all this," he said, rushing over to grab it from her. Her eyes flashed up to his, a pretty hazel flecked with more green than gold, framed by a thick line of black lashes that set her eyes off even more against her dusky skin.

"I'm not a cripple."

Though he'd only known her a week, he was already aware that whatever injury she'd sustained was a touchy issue with her. "I know you're not. But you could hurt yourself more and there's no reason to risk it. Hunt and I've got it covered."

She held his gaze for a moment, annoyance burning in her eyes, then lowered them and huffed out a breath. "I hate sitting around when everyone else is working," she muttered. Her cheeks were flushed and he knew it wasn't simply because she was warm.

"I'll take it out of you when you're healed up, promise. Why don't you head down to the truck and wait there? Hunt and I'll bring down the table and chairs then grab the last of the boxes."

"Yeah, okay." She reluctantly released the suitcase and started for the door, her steps slow and deliberate. Sean squelched his automatic instinct to reach out and steady her, knowing it wouldn't go over well. While it was hard to watch her limp away and not do anything, he respected her need for independence and didn't want to embarrass her further by making a big deal out of it. He held the door open for her though and received a murmured thank you.

When she disappeared into the elevator he turned around to find Hunter standing beside the kitchen table, waiting for him. "What's the story with her, do you know?" Sean asked him.

"No idea." He gripped one end of the table. "Shall we?"

Hunt was such a warm and fuzzy kinda guy.

Sean lifted the other end and together they carted it down to the truck. Zahra was sitting in the passenger seat in the cab with the door open. She was chatting away with Ellis, who strung more words together than Sean had ever heard him use in one conversation and was clearly eating up the chance to talk with her. Lucky bastard.

Three more trips up to the apartment and everything was out. Sean did one last sweep of the place before locking it up and meeting the others down at the U-Haul. Hunter was already at the wheel of the SUV behind it. Ellis was still blabbing away to Zahra. Seriously, what the hell could they possibly be talking about this long? The guy honestly wasn't that interesting. Sean walked up to where Ellis had his arm braced against the open passenger side door and cleared his throat to get his attention.

The sniper turned his head and one side of his mouth lifted in a semi-smirk. "Ready to go?"

"Yeah, how about that? Guess you must've missed us bringing down the last couple of loads, huh?" He said it in good humor, since Sean easily trusted his life to Ellis's observational skills. If anything suspicious had happened, Ellis would've noticed and alerted them immediately.

That annoying-as-hell grin widened. "Guess so."

Sean thrust out his hand, palm up. "Keys."

Ellis frowned. "I'm good driving her."

"Hey, you got the cushy lookout job, I get to drive her. Hand 'em over." He opened and closed his hand.

Shaking his head, Ellis offered Zahra an apologetic look and dumped the keys in Sean's hand.

"See you guys there," Sean said cheerfully. He pushed Ellis out of the way to shut Zahra's door for her and gave her a wink. She smiled and settled back against the seat to wait for him to slide behind the wheel, while Ellis got into the tail SUV with Hunter.

Starting the engine, Sean glanced over at her. Her expression was calm and she was putting on a good show of being relaxed but he knew she was worried. And he didn't blame her. Since the bombing two days ago that had almost killed Gage, the team's second-in-command, they'd all been on edge. At least the lines of pain seemed to have faded around her mouth and eyes. "How're you holding up?" he asked now that they were alone.

"Good." He didn't miss the way her gaze strayed to the side mirror and the view of the apartment building as they drove away.

"Alex vetted this new place himself, so it's secure. Only he, the director and our team knows the location."

"I know. I'll feel better when this is all cleared up though."

"Yeah, we all will. I'll be glad when Gage gets back too. I like the way he runs things with Hunter."

She looked over at him. "Have you heard from him and Claire? Is he healing up okay?" She'd been working at NSA headquarters in Fort Meade when Sean had come in to tell her about the bombing. For fear the rest of the team's locations had been compromised by the mole as well, she had to move to a new place. Knowing how much she treasured her privacy, her boss, Alex had thankfully allowed her to stay alone rather than temporarily live with some of the others.

"Hunt talked to him last night and Gage is doing fine. His hearing's not a hundred percent yet but that's no surprise." Especially considering the tough SOB had been blown up in that explosion at the safe house. "They'll be back Sunday night."

Zahra turned her attention to the road in front of them and shook her head. "Glad he's okay. Man, Claire's been through so much, especially having just lost her brother."

Sean nodded. "Sucks that she has to come back and deal with his estate on top of all this."

"At least she's got Gage. He seems rock solid when it comes to dealing with bad stuff."

"He is. Great guy to work with. What about you? You need to call anyone?" With their current state of heightened security she couldn't divulge what was going on, but the NSA didn't expect them to vanish off the grid completely. As long as they were careful and used discretion, they could still maintain contact with close friends and relatives.

"Just a few friends and I've already told them I'm moving."

No family? He filed that information away, more curious about her than ever.

She got quiet after that and he was pretty sure it was because she didn't want him asking any more personal questions so he made due with small talk during the twenty minute drive to her new place. He pulled up to the townhouse complex in the middle class neighborhood and cut the engine as Hunter and Ellis parked behind them.

"All clear?" Sean asked via his earpiece, just to double check, though he hadn't noticed anything suspicious.

"All clear," Hunter responded. "I'm taking watch this time and you guys can unload the truck."

Not about to argue with the boss, Sean smirked as he climbed out of the truck and went around to open Zahra's door. He helped her down to the sidewalk, taking the opportunity to enjoy the feel of the firm curve of her waist against his fingers and the warm, spicy scent of her perfume. Over the past week that scent had become seductive to him and he'd spent the past few nights fantasizing about what he'd do to her if she ever showed an interest in him as a man rather than just a co-worker. She tried to hide it but from watching her he already knew Zahra was an innately sensual woman.

The hotter fantasies had evolved from him merely fucking her, into a slow, thorough seduction to unlock that sensuality trapped just beneath the surface. He wanted to taste her, watch those gorgeous eyes darken with arousal and need as he unraveled her to the point where she was moaning and panting beneath his hands, his mouth, his body.

"Is there a problem?" she asked.

Realizing he was staring and probably making her more uncomfortable, he forced his gaze away. "No, not at all." Damn, he was supposed to be easing her mind, not thinking about stripping her naked and making her come.

The moment she was steady on her own she pulled away and started up the steps with her cane, her gait stiff and jerky.

The bright red front door opened a moment later and out stepped Alex Rycroft, Zahra's boss and the head of the NSA detail Sean and the other Titanium members answered to. In his early fifties, the former SF NCO was dressed casually in jeans and a button down shirt. His silver gaze swept over both vehicles before landing on Sean and he gave a greeting nod. Looking away from him, Alex focused his attention on Zahra. When he saw the cane his eyes turned glacial for a split second, then his whole face softened with the fond smile he gave her.

"Welcome home, Zahra. Everything's set up and ready for you. Come on in and I'll show you around while the boys move your stuff in." He set a hand on her arm, the gesture protective, and to Sean's surprise she didn't argue as Alex helped her up the concrete steps to the front door.

Oh yeah. If anyone knew Zahra's story, Alex did. And knowing what he did of the man, Sean didn't have a chance in hell of prying it out of him.

CHAPTER TWO

Amir parked his cab at the curb in front of the Hilton Baltimore and got out to unload his passenger's luggage. Once the payment was taken care of he climbed back into the Prius and called dispatch. He sighed as he looked at the digital dashboard clock. Another four hours before he was off shift and the night had been slow so far. At this rate he'd barely clear enough to pay for his fuel and meals for the day.

He was debating on where to go next when his cell phone rang in the front cup holder. Pulling it out, he checked the display but didn't recognize the number and there was no name. "Hello."

"Amir. Peace be upon you," the male voice said in Urdu.

"And upon you," he answered, heart beating a little faster. He couldn't be sure it was *them*, but he didn't know who else would call him by name and speak to him in his native tongue other than his family members. And the number had already told him this caller wasn't contacting him from Pakistan.

"Is this a good time to talk?"

"Yes." Actually the timing couldn't be better.

"We have a job for you. You must go to the pre-arranged place and await further instructions. Understand?"

"Yes, I understand."

"How long do you need to get there?"

"Twenty minutes."

"Good. We'll contact you then." He disconnected before Amir could reply.

Amir's pulse throbbed in his throat as he started the vehicle and headed for the highway, excitement and anticipation bubbling hot in his veins. He'd hoped to be of service to the cause one day but hadn't really expected it to happen so soon…

He took the on-ramp onto the highway and sped toward Baltimore/Washington International airport. At this time of night the traffic was light and he arrived on the beltway well within the twenty minute window he'd given. He stayed on the perimeter road and waited for the call, knowing no one would ever be able to track him as long as he stayed in the "dead zone". The air traffic control tower here overpowered signal interception in this precise area. If anyone was tracking him with a beacon or had planted some sort of listening device in the cab, neither would work. He didn't know exactly how it worked or why it was like that, and he didn't much care.

That dead zone was why he'd been instructed previously to come here and why so many drug and arms dealers chose to do their business here. The taxi he drove only made him look even less suspicious and it also enabled him to navigate his way around the city better than anyone. He had the perfect cover. He just hoped he was capable of delivering whatever it was that the cell wanted.

His phone rang a few minutes later and he didn't bother checking the display when he answered this time. The response was immediate.

"You know of the bombing that happened a few days ago?" the man said in Urdu.

Amir knew all about it, from the news coverage. The suspect had been killed, but no one else. The media had tried to link Mostaffa to the Tehrik-i-Taliban Pakistan cell they were both affiliated with but as far as he knew there had been no further developments in the investigation. Until this moment Amir hadn't been sure of the connection. "Yes."

"There is a group of government security contractors we need eliminated. The last operation failed and we are turning to you because of a special connection to a member affiliated with this team who works for the NSA. Her name is Zahra Gill."

At the mention of that name the hairs on the backs of Amir's arms stood up. "I know of her."

"Yes, we know you do. I assume you understand the connection we mean?"

He did and it astounded him. "I haven't seen Ibrahim in years, not since we attended the same mosque together." Before the man had gone to prison for attempted murder.

"You must go see him. Find out if he can locate her. As of right now she's our best chance of finding the other team members, and with no military or weapons training, she's also the weakest link. She's your first target."

"I'll go see him as soon as I can." He both dreaded and welcomed the meeting. There was no telling how the other man would react, but perhaps Amir would walk away with some useful information. At the very least he could ease his old acquaintance's mind that Allah's will would still be carried out.

"When?"

The urgency in the man's voice didn't escape Amir. The man at the top of this chain wanted it taken care of immediately. "Either tomorrow or the next day, depending on when I can get in to see him."

"Good. Find out what he knows and report back to us. Call the first number I contacted you from, at the place you are now."

Amir agreed and ended the call, barely aware of what was happening around him as he drove on the loop back to the airport. He would stop there and pick up his next fare but he knew that until this assignment was taken care of it was all he would think about. He'd only ever killed a human being during combat before this. But then, this *was* a holy war and he was a soldier of Allah, a true believer. He would do what he must to complete the mission.

Once he found the woman, he knew exactly how he would kill her.

History always had a funny way of repeating itself.

Zahra strode into the conference room at the NSA's headquarters just after lunch, anxious to start work after all the chaos of the past three days. After her hasty move and half-ass attempt at unpacking in her new place last night, she'd taken the morning off to tackle necessary errands. Things like forwarding her mail to a P.O. box and pulling out a stack of cash from her savings account to minimize her electronic footprint until the TTP cell and the threat they posed was neutralized.

The room was empty so she crossed to the long rectangular table, set up her laptop at one end and fired it up. Her right hip twinged a bit in protest as she sat but after a night of ibuprofen and stretching, the worst of the pain was gone.

She'd just opened a file Alex had flagged for priority translation when the glass door opened and Sean walked in. He flashed her that easy smile that sent tingles of feminine awareness through her body and suddenly the room seemed much smaller.

"Hey, how'd the unpacking go?" he asked.

"Pretty good. Just a few boxes left."

"What about your hip?"

"Better, thanks." She tore her eyes away from the mouthwatering sight of those broad shoulders and well-developed chest and nodded at her computer screen. "Was just about to start this bit. Should only take me twenty minutes or so. Do you need any help with more encryption? I feel like I'm out of the loop since everything that happened the other day." The enemy's encryption seemed to be getting more and more sophisticated. Zahra lived for cracking it and exposing their ugly secrets to the intelligence world.

"Finish up your stuff first then let's see where I'm at." Rather than sit across or down from her, he chose the seat right beside her and sank into it, the leather creaking under his weight. His warm, clean scent rose up to tease her, a mix of something woodsy and musky. On him it was sinfully delicious. She could feel his dark gaze on her, hot and intense, and it was all she could do not to squirm in her seat. The attraction was there and it was most definitely mutual, simmering just beneath the surface. Her reaction to him was so visceral and unexpected she didn't know what to do with it.

Alex chose that moment to enter the room along with his assistant, Ruth. The sixty-something woman with the plump curves and chin length bob of silver hair was carrying a platter piled high with dark brown squares that smelled of rich, dark chocolate. Zahra's mouth watered instantly. "You made brownies?" she asked hopefully, sitting up a little taller.

Ruth smiled and set the plate down in the center of the table. "They were a hit the last time I brought them in so I figured you guys could use the fuel since Alex told me you're going to be pulling an all-nighter. I've got fresh coffee brewing in the lounge and a pot of that Earl grey you like," she added.

Zahra eyed Alex and shook her head. "They don't make assistants like her anymore. You're so spoiled."

Alex's silver eyes warmed as he chewed a bite of brownie. "I know. She likes to mother me."

"If I didn't, you'd starve to death," Ruth muttered under her breath as she headed for the door.

Zahra started to reach out a hand to grab a brownie but before she could move Sean's arm shot past hers to snag one for himself. She watched as he bit into it and chewed, then let out a low, appreciative groan that sizzled across every one of her nerve endings. She stared helplessly at his sexy mouth, wondering if he made that exact same sound just before he came deep inside a woman's body. Wondering what his lips and tongue and teeth would feel like on her naked skin. Her lower body tightened in reflex and her nipples went rock hard against the cups of her bra.

"Hungry?"

She jerked her eyes up to his, warmth spreading low in her belly at the wicked glint in his dark gaze, the intimate tone. Was she hungry? *Oh yeah*. More than she'd been since…well, ever. There was something about him that captured her interest and wouldn't let go and it wasn't just sexual. She could've controlled that response easily enough. No, this went deeper. He was smart, he was smooth, and the way he watched her, as if he saw into her, filled her stomach with butterflies. The protective streak he'd shown toward her was merely the icing on that luscious cake.

She could tell he knew what he did to her, and from day one he'd never tried to hide his interest. And while she got the impression he was a bit of a player because of the way he flirted and his supreme confidence in his interactions with women in general, he'd never crossed the line or been unprofessional with her.

Which was kind of a shame, when she thought about it.

Realizing she was staring, she pulled her gaze away from him and took a brownie for herself as the blood rushed to her cheeks. The man unnerved and distracted her whenever he was in the same freaking room. How the hell was she supposed to work with him in such close quarters for the foreseeable future? She'd never survive it.

"Hunter and Ellis are out doing surveillance on a possible suspect linked to the TTP cell," Alex told her from across the table where he was setting down stacks of files in front of him. "Dunphy's going to keep working on breaking the encryption to the new forum we found the other night while you finish up digging through the messages I sent you. If anything looks suspicious, flag it and I'll take a look. We know Hassani's got more people willing to carry out attacks here on his behalf and we know the TTP is in tight with him. They've likely got something else already in the works and we're going to follow it right up the chain of communication and find this bastard before he can do any more damage."

"Got it. Haven't found anything suspicious yet but I'm only halfway through the translations." Some of them were in Urdu, some were in Pashto. She typed the English beneath the lines while Alex left the room. Sean was busy typing on his own laptop. With him so close it was hard not to keep glancing over at him and she had to work at concentrating on the task at hand.

Alex strode back in a few minutes later and helped himself to another brownie. Stuffing half of it into his mouth, he lifted his eyebrows at her in question. Zahra frowned, not understanding. "What?" she asked when he kept staring at her expectantly.

He nodded at Sean. "You ask him yet?"

Sean lifted his head. "Ask me what?"

Zahra sent her boss a warning look, but Alex just grinned and swallowed the last mouthful of brownie. "She needs a date for Saturday night."

Zahra wanted to close her eyes and cover her burning face with her hands as Sean turned his head and his dark gaze focused on her. "That right?"

"She's getting some big alumni award from MIT for her encryption work here. Not that they really have a clue what goes on inside these walls," Alex continued, eyes full of amusement at her discomfort. "The event's black tie, very swanky. In light of the security situation she was thinking of not going, but then she asked me what I thought of taking you with her."

She opened her mouth to protest, say something in her defense, but Alex just kept going.

"I told her as long as she took one of you guys as a precaution, she should go. You up for it?"

Sean was still staring at her, expression unreadable. "Were you going to ask me yourself?"

God, now she looked like a total moron *and* a wuss. She shifted in her chair and cleared her throat, avoiding his gaze as she glared at Alex. Her reluctance about attending wasn't just because of the current security threat and he knew it. He knew about her past, knew exactly why she kept to herself. That single, horrific incident had shattered her life and she doubted she'd ever feel truly safe again. "I just wanted his opinion on whether I should go or not, because of everything that's going on," she clarified.

"She was working up the guts to ask you, but I wanted to make sure it was out there in case she wimped out," Alex finished helpfully. "The award's a big deal, I wouldn't want her to miss it and with the other guys out on surveillance this was as good a time as any to bring it up."

The glacial glare she was sending his way had absolutely no effect. His usual bluntness was way over the top this time though. She knew he was fond of her. Since he'd hired her he'd taken on the role of a kind of protective father figure in her life and she knew it was because of her background. He'd been very thorough in his research before he'd approached her for recruitment and hadn't pulled any punches when he'd finally questioned her about her past in the initial interview.

While horrific, that same past had galvanized her to do whatever she could to help stamp out radical Islam wherever it showed its ugly face, something Alex also knew. That trait was probably a huge reason why he'd hired her, aside from her degree from MIT. Presented with a position to eradicate some of the evil in this world, she'd jumped at the chance and worked her ass off for him ever since.

Sean still hadn't taken his eyes off her, his dark gaze intent. "Do you want me to take you, Zahra?"

Take her. The words, spoken in that low, smoky voice, shot an image into her brain of them together. Naked. Her pinned beneath his hard weight in her queen size bed. That powerful body stretched out on top of her, her hands locked on his wide, muscular back as he devoured her mouth and pumped in and out of her in a rhythm that made her whimper and strain for more.

She swallowed, risked a glance over at him. He was watching her closely, studying her reaction in that intent way of his and she couldn't do anything to hide the damned blush currently burning in her cheeks. "If you wouldn't mind, I'd really appreciate it." She'd feel a helluva lot safer with him there to keep watch, that was for sure, insane physical reaction to him notwithstanding.

Those espresso eyes filled with a lazy sensuality, the dark chocolate flecks in them visible as he smiled. "Then it's a date. Is it black tie as in I'll need a tux?"

She nodded, her mouth going dry. The man was ruggedly gorgeous in jeans and a T-shirt. She couldn't even imagine what the sight of him in a tux would do to her. And she knew without a doubt that he'd spend the evening being very attentive to her. Her body went hot all over at the thought and made her question her sanity. Was this a huge mistake?

"Great," Alex said decisively. "Glad that's settled. Now if you don't mind, could you guys get back to work?"

Zahra expelled a breath and shot him one last narrow-eyed look before opening the next document on her laptop, every cell in her body humming with a constant physical reminder of how close Sean was. All she had to do now was figure out a way to ignore that long enough to get her job done and not think about being alone with him two nights from now.

CHAPTER THREE

Seated at the conference room table, Sean sent off another file to Alex. With Zahra's help he'd just hacked into yet another terrorist forum and uncovered all kinds of chatter that needed translation. One item down, another thousand to go.

After a long day of surveillance, Hunter and Ellis had finally come back to the office an hour ago to report on their findings. So far neither of the suspects they'd tailed had done anything worrisome, but they'd remain on the watch list along with several other men Zahra's translations had flagged from the jihadist forums she'd been looking at all day. Alex wrapped the meeting up by announcing no further progress in the FBI's findings, but stressed the recent chatter suggested another plot was well underway. Though they couldn't be sure of the target, due to the recent bombing at the safe house they could safely assume they were all still at the top of that hit list.

Sean stood up and stretched his arms over his head to work out the stiffness in his muscles from sitting at the computer all day. Since it was now well past dinner time everyone was starving and they'd long since run out of Ruth's brownies, so he volunteered to run out and grab them all something to eat.

When he walked in half an hour later carrying takeout, the mood was still serious and a little tense. That was about to change, however. It'd been a while since he'd pulled a decent prank on his teammates and he was long overdue with these guys. He had a reputation to uphold, after all.

Zahra glanced up at him with a tired smile, her eyes lighting up. "You brought food! That makes you my new favorite person."

He loved seeing that smile on her too often serious face, and knowing he was the cause of it. "Well damn, if I'd known it was that easy to charm you I'd have done this days ago." He set the bags and drink trays down on the table. Hunter, Ellis and Alex all stopped what they were doing and started converging on it like a pack of starving wolves. "Ah ah ah." Sean staved them off with an upraised hand. "Ladies first."

They glanced at Zahra and eased back to wait and he saw her lips quirk. By the color rising to her cheeks he knew that the little show of courtesy had surprised and pleased her. He couldn't remember the last time a woman had intrigued him this much. The only thing that kept him from digging into her background was knowing how much she'd resent that, and besides, he wanted her to tell him what had happened on her own. He already knew she didn't trust easily, so snooping into her past would damage things between them before they'd even begun.

Opening the first bag, he pulled out her sandwich wrapped in white paper and offered it to her. "Chicken, grilled, and a salad instead of fries. Dressing on the side."

She quirked one black eyebrow as he handed it all to her. "My, you really do pay attention."

"Yes, ma'am." More than she realized. He was determined to learn everything he could about her, discover what made her tick, what made her melt and what turned her on.

Once he did, he planned to put all that information to good use. The repressed desire he sensed in her made him want to stake his claim on her in any way she'd let him.

Shoving those distracting thoughts away, he dug into the other bags. "All right, the rest of us get spicy burgers and fries." As he passed them out he noticed Zahra reaching for one of the sodas in the cardboard tray.

"Here, take this one," he said, brushing her hand aside and carefully selecting the one closest to him. She accepted it with a murmured thanks and a questioning look he didn't respond to as he doled out the drinks to the others.

"You get cheese on these?" Hunter asked, already unwrapping his burger and dumping his fries onto the paper alongside it.

"Yep, and bacon too. Figured I'd go all out, you know?"

"Thanks, 'cuz I'm starving," Ellis muttered, dropping into a chair across from him and opening up the wrapper.

Alex reached out for a soda. "Coke?" he asked Sean.

"Pepsi." Sean handed them some napkins before helping himself to the last burger he'd placed at the bottom of the bag. He sat, shifting so that the little bottle hidden in his pocket didn't dig into his hip.

Alex made a face at the Pepsi announcement but didn't say anything as he sat beside Hunter, who was in between him and Ellis.

Hiding a grin, Sean pulled his chair in and moved it close enough to Zahra's that he could nudge her foot with his. She looked over at him questioningly with her chicken sandwich poised halfway to her delectable mouth. She had the prettiest smile, all the more gorgeous because it was rare, and he hoped this would get him another one. He gave a subtle tilt of his head toward the others and her gaze flicked to the men across the table. Picking up his own burger, Sean bit into it and chewed, prepared to enjoy the show.

"Spicy," he said around a mouthful, then picked up his soda and took a sip, never taking his eyes off the others.

Ellis had been the first to bite into his burger. He chewed a couple of times then stopped, seemed to roll the food around in his mouth for a second before he suddenly sped up and gulped it down, looking like someone was strangling him. He glanced at the burger then cast a sidelong look at Hunter, who was frowning as he chewed his own mouthful. Alex was far less subtle. His face was screwed up in pain as he forced the bite down his throat then let out a cough.

"Hot?" Sean asked casually, taking another bite and chewing slowly before sipping more of his drink.

Alex nodded, staring at his burger in suspicion.

"Try some soda. The sugar takes the burn away."

All three men reached for their drinks at once and took a long draw through their straws. A second later they all started choking and spluttering, spraying soda all over the table. Their faces were red, sweat beading on their brows. Beside him, Zahra had set her sandwich down, her eyes wide as she stared at them.

It was all he could do not to burst out laughing when three pairs of angry eyes locked on him from across the table. Alex snatched up a napkin and scrubbed at his mouth, nailing him with a glare so hostile it should've melted his face right off. "You fucker," he breathed.

"Asshole," spat Hunter.

Realizing what he'd done, Zahra lashed out with one hand and smacked him on the upper arm. "Sean," she admonished, but her eyes were dancing. Her lips trembled as if she was fighting a smile, then they curved upwards and ah, yeah, there it was. Beautiful. Totally worth the effort and whatever retribution he'd face later for this little stunt.

One of the guys let out a loud curse and he couldn't hold it in anymore. Laughing, rather pleased with himself, Sean bit into his burger and made a show of savoring the mouthful before he swallowed, keeping his expression innocent.

"Not cool, man," Ellis wheezed, mopping at his sweaty face with a paper napkin.

Nope, not cool at all. Try flamethrower hot, Sean thought with glee.

Ellis chuckled despite himself even as he wiped at the moisture on his upper lip. "All right, you got us, douchenozzle. That was a pretty good one."

"I enjoyed it," he replied, taking another sip of the cool, sweet soda as he surveyed the damage he'd inflicted.

Hunter was still glaring a hole through his face. Sean met his gaze, lifted an eyebrow and kept eating, so Hunter picked up his nuclear hot burger and defiantly took another bite, managing to hide a wince as the hot sauce seared his taste buds. Pranks were common in the Spec Ops community—hell, the entire military community—so he wasn't that surprised by Hunter's *fuck you* response.

Ellis chuckled and shook his head at him. "That's hardcore, man, even for an ex-SEAL. Hardcore."

Hunter forced the bite down his throat and picked up his soda for a long pull, trying his best not to give away how much pain he was in. Sean grinned and raised his cup in acknowledgement. "Cheers, man." The team leader was one tough sonofabitch. Sean appreciated and respected his leadership.

"How the hell can you drink that?" Alex demanded with a shake of his head, his expression one of combined awe and disgust.

"Have to," Hunter muttered, wiping at his sweaty face with the back of one arm. "Gotta show the little bastard who's toughest."

"Be my guest," Sean said and kicked back in his chair to polish off his dinner while he watched Hunter suffer in silence. "Fries are safe though, for the rest of you wusses. Had to leave you something edible."

Taking pity on the others, Zahra handed over her drink to Ellis and left the room, reappearing a minute later with some bottled water. She unscrewed the top off one and held it out to Hunter. He was sweating profusely, his face bright red. He took it with a nod of thanks and proceeded to eat every last bite of his burger before allowing himself a single sip of water. The rest of them sat back and watched him try not to sputter as he choked the last bite down.

"What the hell was in that hot sauce, napalm?" he rasped out, tilting his head back to drain the water bottle in three gulps.

Sean drew the bottle of hot sauce out of his pocket and held it up for inspection. "Ghost peppers," he replied with an evil grin. "Over a million Scoville Heat Units each."

"Fuck yeah, they are," Hunter retorted. "I've got third degree burns down my esophagus."

"That's because you just had to win the alpha male pissing contest by eating the *whole thing*," Zahra pointed out with a laugh.

Hunter's harsh face cracked into a grin. "Yeah. I'm the man."

"You're the man," Sean agreed with a chuckle.

Hunter's eyes zeroed in on him once more and the evil smile that transformed his face gave Sean a moment's unease. "Wait for it, Dunphy. Payback's a bitch, especially the way I dish it out."

Oh, it was so on.

Delighted, Sean grinned at the threat and got busy helping clean up. He'd lightened the mood, provided a few minutes of entertainment and made Zahra smile, so mission accomplished on all fronts. Now they could buckle down and refocus for another few hours. Hunter might want a handful of antacids first, though.

Sean went over some intel on a few possible terror cell suspects in the Baltimore/DC area with the others, Zahra clarifying any fine points in the translation between English and Urdu or Pashto. The FBI had teams out doing surveillance on some suspects already, so Sean and the other Titanium members would take up the slack on the new leads. It was almost midnight by the time they called it a night and headed home.

Hunter and Ellis took one SUV and Sean drove the other, following Zahra's red compact car to her new place. She unlocked the front door and waved to him from the steps before disappearing inside and shutting it. Arriving at the modest suburban house he now shared with Hunter and Ellis, he parked at the curb and walked up the driveway. He was careful on his way inside, half expecting some sort of booby trap or ambush by Hunter. When he was sure it was all clear he jogged up the carpeted stairs to his room and gave it the same thorough inspection before stepping inside, even checking beneath the bed and covers before crawling in.

He was safe for the moment, but provoking an ex-SEAL like Hunter probably hadn't been his best idea. Sean knew one thing for sure; when Hunt finally made his move, it would be epic. Sick as it sounded, he couldn't wait to find out what it would be.

Zahra's eyes snapped open in the darkness. She laid there, heart pounding, wondering if she'd had another nightmare or if something else had woken her. A thin slice of light filtered in from the master ensuite door she'd left open a crack, illuminating the foreign landscape of her new bedroom. The digital clock on her nightstand read just after two in the morning. Nothing moved in the stillness and there was no noise from downstairs.

A thump sounded outside her bedroom window.

She came up on her elbows and froze like that, willing the cold prickle of fear to recede as she tried to determine whether that thump signalled some sort of threat. There was a smaller thump, then a soft scraping sound against the side of the townhouse, below her second floor window.

Throwing back the covers, she jumped out of bed and pulled out the bedside table drawer to grab the Taser Alex had given her when she'd moved in. As an analyst she had no weapons training at all, had never fired this or any other weapon before but he'd told her in an emergency to just point and pull the trigger. She could definitely manage that if it came down to it.

Gripping the weapon tight she ran downstairs to the living room as quickly as her stiff right hip would allow. On the wall next to the front door, the alarm system keypad blinked at her, telling her it was still armed. The large window facing the street was covered by venetian blinds so she carefully lifted the edge and peeked outside.

Four cars were parked on the street in front of her unit. Someone sat in the driver's seat of one of them. She was just about to release the blind when a man appeared in her peripheral vision, walking away from the front of her unit toward the car. She ducked down so he wouldn't see her and stared, holding her breath as she took in his appearance with the help of the streetlight. Thirtyish, short dark hair, black leather jacket and jeans. She couldn't see his face or anything else that might help her remember him. It might have been her imagination but she thought she saw a bulge in the back of his waistband, as if he had a weapon concealed there. Zahra's fingers curled into the edge of the blind.

He leaned into the open passenger window to say something to the driver, then straightened and looked back over his shoulder at her place. Zahra braced for action, ready to snatch her phone from the kitchen and call 911 if he tried to break in. He seemed to be studying something on the front of her unit. After a few seconds he opened the passenger door and climbed in. The engine started and the driver steered away from the curb. Frozen in place, Zahra kept her gaze trained on the red glow of the tail lights until they disappeared from view down the street. She waited a few minutes to see if they came back. Had they been casing her place? Searching for something, maybe a way in?

She let the blinds go and eased back to sit with her back propped up against the wall. It was possible she was overreacting and being completely paranoid.

It was also possible the terror cell had somehow traced her here and was planning some sort of attack.

Pressing a hand to her racing heart, she debated her options. Since it was the middle of the night she couldn't call one of her friends and ask them to come over. Plus if there really was some sort of threat brewing she didn't want to put them at risk. She could get in her car and drive somewhere else, but if anyone was watching or following her it would make her an easy, isolated target.

Both Alex and Hunter had stressed that she should report anything suspicious, so she headed for the darkened kitchen where she'd left her cell charging on the counter and dialed Sean's number.

He picked up after the second ring, his voice clear and alert as though he'd already been awake. "Zahra?"

"Yeah, hi." She ran a hand through her hair and fought back the embarrassment creeping over her. "Listen, sorry to bother you but I was wondering if you could come by and check out my place."

He was silent a moment. "Did something happen?"

"I'm not exactly sure, but…" She detailed what had happened and gave him the license plate of the vehicle. "If they were up to no good and trying to find a way in, maybe the alarm put them off?"

"I'll be over in fifteen minutes," he said. "Wait where you are and don't turn on any lights. Don't open the door for anyone but one of us, got it?"

"Got it." She set her cell back down on the counter and dropped into the chair she'd placed at the computer nook, blowing out a hard breath. The air conditioning wasn't on but the place was cool and with the tile floor it was downright cold in here. She rubbed her hands over her bare upper arms then curled her arms around her knees to wait.

There were no more noises, nothing suspicious until she heard a vehicle pull up about fifteen minutes later. Footsteps came up the walkway and then a soft knock sounded at the front door. She got up and checked the peephole, shocked by how relieved she felt when she saw Sean standing there. She disabled the alarm, unlocked the door and swung it open.

Her breath caught at the sight of him in his leather jacket. "Hi," she said softly, feeling stupid now that everything was fine and that she'd dragged him out of bed in the middle of the night for nothing.

"Hey," he responded, face grim as he swept his eyes over her thin tank and pajama pants then up to her face. "You all right?"

"I'm fine." Her gaze dropped to his hands and she realized with a start that he was holding a gun. She'd expected him to be armed, but not literally holding a weapon. She automatically put a hand to her throat and took a step back, fighting the instinctive leap of fear that shot a surge of adrenaline into her system.

Noting her reaction, Sean angled his body away so she wasn't openly confronted by the pistol. Though he couldn't possibly understand the reason for her fear, she was once again grateful for his perception and thoughtfulness. "Ellis is doing a sweep around back," he said. "As soon as we're done we're going to check the inside of the house, okay?"

She nodded, understanding it was procedure and common sense to be this careful if she'd called him here at this hour.

"Wait in the downstairs bathroom and shut the door. I'll come get you after I make sure everything's still secure, okay?"

"Okay." She closed the front door behind him and went to the powder room as he'd told her. She waited in there until his voice carried to her from the front entry.

"It's just us, Zahra. You still good?"

"Yes," she called back, feeling more stupid than ever.

A few minutes later there was a knock on the bathroom door and she opened it to see Sean there. "Everything's good," he told her, and the residual ball of tension in her stomach eased. He turned his head and spoke to Ellis, somewhere behind him. "See you in the morning, man." The front door shut and Sean went over to it. Zahra came out of the bathroom in time to see him lock it and turn back to face her. He was staying? The idea both thrilled and embarrassed her. She didn't want him thinking that she was some head case afraid of her own shadow.

"We ran that plate number and there were no hits but Hunter's going to check up on the registered owner just in case," he told her, taking off his jacket to expose a shoulder holster. He did something to the weapon—putting on the safety maybe?—holstered it and shrugged it off his body, handling each movement with the ease of a man who'd spent the majority of his adult life in the military.

Zahra wiped a hand down the side of her face and sighed, glad the gun was out of sight. "Sorry," she muttered. "I woke out of a dead sleep when I heard that noise and wasn't sure what was going on."

Sean shrugged. "Better to be safe than sorry, and it's weird that anyone would be skulking around your place at this time of night."

His phrasing amused her. "Skulking?"

He grinned, his white teeth flashing in the light coming from the bathroom behind her. "Yeah. It's a technical recon term." He raked his gaze down the length of her again, this time taking in the shape of her body and the way her nipples, hard from the cool air and his perusal, pressed against the thin cotton of the tank top.

She folded her arms across her breasts, suddenly self-conscious and berating herself for the wave of heat that spread beneath her skin at the frank male interest in his eyes. "Can I get you something? I feel terrible for dragging you over here now."

"Nah, I'm good. And don't worry about it—we'll both sleep better now that we know nothing's going on."

He was so gorgeous and strong and he'd rushed straight over here to make sure she was safe. Not only that, he was staying to make sure she remained that way. Again, that show of protectiveness melted her.

To cover her reaction and growing attraction to him, she gestured toward the living room. "I guess you remember I don't have a bed in the guest room. The pullout in there's all I have." She nodded to the couch set beneath the front window.

"That's fine. Mind if I set it up?"

"No, go ahead. I'll just grab you a pillow and blankets." She rushed upstairs to the linen closet in the hallway and came back with a pillow, fitted sheet and a comforter. Sean had the bed pulled out of the frame and took the sheet from her. She helped him stretch it over the lumpy mattress and fluffed the comforter before spreading it over the top. "Not the best bed in the world but I hope it won't be too uncomfortable."

He gave her a slow smile that sent her pulse up a few notches. "I've slept in much worse, I promise. This is great."

She tossed him the pillow. "So I guess all of us are gonna be tired tomorrow because of me, huh?"

"Nah, Hunt was still awake when I came downstairs. Apparently he's got a bad case of heartburn because I caught him with a half empty bottle of Tums." His grin was full of mischief.

"Gee, I wonder why?"

"It was awesome," he said on a chuckle, totally unrepentant. Then he faced her and put his hands on his lean hips, the pose emphasizing the muscles in his arms and shoulders. "You want to try and get more sleep now?"

She shook her head, knowing she was too wired to sleep. "I'm wide awake, but you go ahead. I'll just watch a movie in the other room for a bit until I get tired."

"I'll watch one with you," he said and strode for the kitchen and the family room off to the side where the TV was set up. Surprised, she didn't move until he looked back at her and quirked a brow, a hint of challenge in his dark eyes. "Coming?"

Scared? that look said, his tone daring her to chicken out.

Sensing she was asking for complications she wasn't certain she was ready for, Zahra nodded and followed him anyway.

CHAPTER FOUR

Zahra chose an action flick, though Sean would've gladly suffered through a chick flick if it meant being able to sit next to her right now, alone. She was curled up into the arm of the couch, wrapped up in a throw blanket, and he wondered if it was because she felt safer that way around him.

Already spooked by whatever those guys had been up to, he'd seen the look on her face when she'd noticed him holding his SIG. She'd blanched and her pupils had constricted. A lot of people outside of law enforcement or military were uncomfortable around weapons, he got that, but her reaction had been one of fear on a gut deep level. Weird, considering she worked for the NSA, because surely she must have been around enough people carrying since she'd been there, especially at the Fort Meade building. He'd noticed the Taser she'd left on the kitchen counter. It wasn't nearly enough protection for her.

The room was sparsely furnished and she only had a few knickknacks out. A framed picture of her and who he assumed must be her mother sat in a niche beside the mantel. Zahra looked a little younger in it, her long dark hair falling around her shoulders, the older woman wearing a headscarf traditional for Pakistani women. "Is that your mother?" he asked her.

Zahra looked over at him, followed his gaze to the picture. "Yes." She shifted and fixed her attention back on the movie, her expression stiff.

Knowing he was treading on shaky ground, he couldn't help asking, "Does she live in Baltimore?"

"No. She died a few years ago," she said quietly.

He hid a wince. "Sorry." He wanted to ask what had happened but from her clipped tone and they way she avoided his gaze, sensed he'd better not.

She sighed and relaxed. "Thanks. What about you?" This time she turned to face him.

"My parents are still married and I've got an older brother who's a firefighter. They live in Coeur d'Alene, where I grew up."

She seemed intrigued by that. "I always wanted a sibling."

Sean made a face. "It's overrated," he teased.

She tilted her head. "You're not close with him?"

"Yeah, we're pretty tight. I mean, we had our moments growing up where my mom had to intervene to stop us from beating the shit out of each other, but that's normal brother stuff." He waved his hand dismissively. "He's married with a little girl and another baby on the way. My mom's ecstatic, of course. I'm due for a visit home soon. Been over six months since I was there."

"Do you talk to them often at least?" She seemed concerned that he wasn't being a good son and brother.

"Every week at least, sometimes more."

"That's good." She brought her knees up and focused on the blanket as she shifted it over her body. "My mom and I were really close. We talked every day and saw each other a few times a month after I moved out."

Sean noticed she had yet to mention her father at all.

"Why did you go into the Marine Corps?"

He blinked at the sudden change of subject but went with it. "Because it's the coolest." He got a small smile for that. "Family tradition, for one. My grandpa, great grandpa and one uncle all served in the Corps. It's all I ever wanted to do. Well, I always knew I wanted to make Force Recon one day."

"Did you love it like you thought you would?"

"Yeah. Mostly I loved the guys. Still miss 'em."

"When did you know it was time to get out?" she asked, setting her chin atop her upraised knees.

"I'd had my fill of eating dust and being so hard on my body. We lost some of our best guys, others left and I knew it was time to go. Losing your buddies, that stays with you, you know?" He still thought about them often and some days were better than others. The things he'd seen...even time couldn't erase that.

She nodded, and from the empathy in her eyes he felt like she truly did understand. "And did you start working for Titanium right away?"

"No, I'd been out for almost a year before I applied with Tom." Tom Webster, former SEAL and co-owner of Titanium Security.

"What did you do in the interim?"

"Drank."

She blinked at the blunt way he said it, but it was the truth and trust was a two-way street so he felt obligated to be honest with her about this. He wasn't proud of his past behavior.

"Yeah, I drank every day, and way too much. My brother eventually pointed out that I was becoming a full blown alcoholic and dragged me to AA. I was in denial at first, of course. He went with me for the first month, made sure I understood that I had a problem, then made sure I stuck it out."

"I'm glad he was there for you. And so...how are you doing with it now?"

"Good. I've got a two beer limit and never touch the hard stuff. Looking back it was mostly a combination of feeling lost, some boredom and dealing with the shit I'd seen. I'm not bored or lost anymore and since I've been sober the rest of it's eased up too."

Rather than appear disappointed in him for being a drunk, those sweetly curved lips tilted upward as she sat up and leaned back against the couch, closer to him this time. "Good."

Stupid to feel warmed by her praise, but he couldn't deny the warmth it unfurled inside him. "Thanks."

Zahra turned her attention back to the movie but the earlier discomfort he'd sensed from her was gone. She still had the blanket on, the top of it just covering her breasts. He could smell her though, clean and sweet and female. Her left arm was almost touching his right one and he could feel the warmth of her skin on his. He'd seen the feminine interest in her eyes sometimes when she looked at him. He'd been with his fair share of women. With any other woman he wouldn't hesitate to lean over, take her chin in one hand and tip her head back to kiss her. With Zahra he couldn't tell what her reaction would be and that stopped him cold.

They watched the movie in silence together but Sean wasn't paying much attention to what was happening on screen, and what he did notice made him want to roll his eyes. He was much more interested in Zahra and what to do about the unfamiliar situation he now found himself in.

Using some of the skills he'd mastered during countless stalks in the Corps, he used tiny, imperceptible movements to inch closer to her without her noticing. A few minutes later when she raised a hand to yawn their shoulders bumped. She glanced up at him in surprise then smiled. Sean took that as an invitation and stretched an arm across her shoulders. Rather than stiffen or pull away Zahra leaned into him with a little sigh, and that simple show of trust tightened something in his gut. He *wanted* her to lean on him, turn to him for comfort or sex or anything else she needed.

Anything but friend-zoning him, that is.

She settled against his side and he savored the feel of her trim curves pressed along his ribs. Keeping his eyes on the movie he toyed with the ends of her hair, sliding his fingers through the silky soft strands. In answer she made a quiet humming sound and rested her head in the hollow of his shoulder.

"Thanks for coming over," she whispered.

"You're welcome," he whispered back, bending to press a kiss to the top of her head. Straightening, he noticed her eyes were closed and a tiny, secret smile was on her lips. More than anything he wanted to settle his mouth over hers to taste her, learn every last one of her secrets. He stayed where he was, content for now to have her cuddled into him so trustingly.

The movie wore on but she didn't open her eyes. Her breathing grew deeper, slower, and her body leaned into him more heavily. When he was sure she was asleep Sean reached for the remote beside her and shut the TV off. With the room plunged into darkness he eased her even closer until her head rested on his chest, leaned back and allowed himself to doze, his arm still wrapped around her.

He wasn't sure how much time had passed when the buzzing of his cell phone woke them both. Zahra came awake with a rush and sat up as he pulled the phone from his pocket to see it was Hunter calling. He answered and listened to the info Hunt gave him then hung up and put the phone away.

"Everything okay?" Zahra asked hesitantly, watching him, her face washed in the pale moonlight streaming in from the kitchen windows behind them.

"Yeah, it's fine. Hunter got a call about that car's registered owner. One of the guys who was here was a former informant in an arms dealer case for the NSA. Apparently he lived here until a few weeks ago and stopped by to pick up something he'd left behind." No doubt weapons, drugs or cash he'd hidden somewhere. "His handler talked to him an hour ago. The guy didn't realize the place was occupied again but he got what he wanted so he won't be back."

"Oh. Weird." She tucked a lock of hair behind her ear, frowning. The blanket had fallen away from her body, revealing the curves of her breasts, the outline of her nipples that were now hard. Small breasts, but he'd bet they were sensitive and would fit perfectly in his palms and mouth.

She looked down at the arm he still had draped across her shoulders. "Sorry I fell asleep on you."

"I'm not."

Her gaze flew up to his and locked there. In the pale moonlight he clearly saw the way her pupils dilated. Sean lifted the hand on her shoulder to stroke the hair away from her face, fascinated when that light touch raised goose bumps along her bare skin. She licked her lips to say something, looked like she was going to move away, but didn't. "I should let you up so you can sleep on a proper bed."

"I'm good right here." He didn't stop stroking her hair and though he wanted to stroke so much more, he knew it was too soon.

He could see the pulse point beating in her throat as she hesitated. He wanted to nuzzle her there with his nose and lips, slowly, so she could feel the heat of his breath then caress that sensitive hollow with his tongue and feel her shiver in reaction.

"Stretch out here with me," he coaxed, locking down the lust raging inside him. "It's plenty wide for both of us."

She seemed so uncertain as she studied him, likely wondering if he was going to push her for more. As much as he'd kill for the chance, he wouldn't ask her for anything she wasn't ready to give. "Just to sleep," he assured her, still playing with her hair. "I like the feel of you snuggled up against me." The physical proof was pressed hard against the fly of his jeans if she'd cared to look, except what he felt for her was more than just lust. He wanted to unlock the secrets shadowing her hazel eyes, have her reach for him, let him unfurl her like a flower opening to the sun.

He was sure she was going to laugh him off or refuse him outright but she surprised him by giving a little nod and that secretive smile he wanted to taste so badly. Giving her no time to change her mind, Sean stretched out with his back along the length of the couch and tugged her into place in front of him. With her hips and spine resting against his front he spread the blanket over them, slid one arm beneath her neck and wrapped the other around her waist, his face tucked into her nape. She was stiff for a moment before she exhaled and relaxed into his body.

Savoring the victory, Sean closed his eyes and enjoyed the feel of her pressed so close to him, careful to keep a few inches of space between her hips and his aching erection. Wrapped around Zahra, keeping her safe and warm and relaxed, he listened to her breathing shift as she fell asleep and knew there was nowhere on earth he'd rather be.

Zahra woke when someone shifted behind her. She jerked awake, her eyes flying open and realized it was Sean's strong arm wrapped around her. The scent of coffee tickled her nose. Blinking in the bright morning light flooding the room from the kitchen windows, she went dead still when she felt the thick, hard ridge of his morning erection pressed against her backside.

The thick forearm curled around her stomach tightened briefly and she felt him press a kiss to the back of her head. "Morning."

That soft, sleepy tone was just as intimate as their position. For just a moment Zahra closed her eyes and allowed herself to soak in the feel of him so warm and solid and hungry against her. Her breasts tightened against the fabric of her tank top and a slow pulse throbbed between her legs. If she arched a bit she could rub the lower curve of her breast against the top of that muscled forearm. She wanted him to slide his hand beneath her top so she could feel it against her bare skin, have him glide it upward until he cupped her breast and brushed his thumb over the aching peak. The dampening flesh between her thighs felt swollen, that unfulfilled ache impossible to ignore. She moved slightly and pressed her legs together to ease the sensation but it didn't help.

He squeezed her once then let go. "It's almost eight. We'd better get ready and head into work."

Right. Fantasy shattered, Zahra pushed up into a sitting position and stood, avoiding his gaze as she wrapped her arms around herself and headed for the hallway. With her hair down and the tank top covering most of her back, she doubted he could see her scars and it had been so dark last night there was no way he could've noticed them. She wasn't ashamed of them, but she wasn't ready for the questions they'd inevitably cause.

"Coffee's already made if you want some," she said over her shoulder, glad she'd remembered to program the coffee maker the night she'd moved in. "Grab a shower in the guest bath if you want one."

She fled up the stairs, her body reminding her with every step how unhappy it was for denying it the opportunity to explore the unprecedented arousal flooding her. With the act of simply waking up to find herself held so securely against his muscular body, Sean had managed to get her hotter than any of the guys she'd actually slept with.

After showering and dressing in a charcoal gray pencil skirt and fitted pale pink long sleeved top, she blow dried her hair and twisted it up into a knot at the back of her head so it wouldn't get in her way. She brushed her teeth, put on a little eye makeup and hurried back down to the kitchen. Sean stood leaning against the counter, his hair damp from a recent shower, those muscles filling out his T-shirt every bit as well as she remembered.

"Did you leave any for me?" she asked because she couldn't think of anything better to say.

"One cup, black, two sugars," he responded, sliding a steaming mug toward her.

She shook her head at him, smiling as she took it. "You remembered."

"I'm good with details," he answered, eyes sparkling with innuendo.

Still remembering the feel of him imprinted against her body, she forced her gaze away from those dark, hypnotic eyes and headed for the garage. "Shall we?"

The commute was comfortable though Zahra couldn't help stealing glances at him as she drove. Another lifetime ago she'd have been all over the chance to have sex with him. She wasn't the same person she'd been back in college though.

Hookups hadn't been all that satisfying to begin with and without some sort of reciprocated emotional component she wasn't interested in sleeping with anyone, not even Sean. Though thinking of how he'd held her all night made her feel all fluttery inside. If he met her even partway, she could see herself falling for him, hard. Then she'd just have to hope she wasn't merely a conquest for him to make.

They rode the elevator up and exited at the hallway leading to Alex's office. Ruth was at her desk typing away and smiled when she saw them.

"Is he in a meeting?" Zahra asked her.

Ruth's expression became pinched and she looked away before answering. "He's doing more interviews this morning. He and Evers have been taking turns with the questioning."

To find the mole within the NSA, she meant, with Jake Evers, the FBI agent assisting Alex. The NSA had teamed up with the FBI to work behind the scenes going over phone call transcripts, computer searches and whatnot, making certain that all the employees checked out clean for involvement with a terror cell.

"Two more to go, then it's my turn in the hot seat," Ruth finished, rubbing her hands against her skirt.

Zahra smiled in encouragement. "It's just standard procedure. We've all been grilled already. You'll do fine. Don't let him bully you though," she added with a wink.

"Got any more of those brownies?" Sean asked hopefully beside her, scanning the desk, his face falling a little when he didn't see a plate among the pictures of Ruth's son, daughter-in-law and three grandchildren.

"Sorry, got home too late last night to make a new batch. Maybe tomorrow."

"Only if you have time," Sean said with a dismissive wave.

"Well, better you guys eat them than me. Another few weeks of this stress and I won't fit into any of my clothes."

"You look great," Zahra told her, and grabbed Sean's arm to tow him away. "See you after your interview."

"Okay."

"You've got a sweet tooth, huh?" Zahra noted as they headed down the carpeted hallway to the conference room.

"Not just one," he argued. "Can't help it though. I love sweet things."

At the sensual tone she stopped to look over her shoulder at him and was unsurprised to see the hunger burning there. Her pulse tripped and her mouth went dry before she shook herself and faced forward once more. "Don't distract me while I'm working, Dunphy."

"Sorry, can't promise you that, *Gill*."

The man was such trouble. She got a kick out of his playfulness. Hiding a smile, she entered the conference room to find Hunter and Ellis already at work on some new files. "Morning. Got anything new for me to work on?"

Hunter straightened. "Yeah, a couple. Alex is gonna be busy for another few hours yet, so he told us to go out and do some more surveillance. You up for it?"

Her? Surveillance? "Sure, but I've never—"

"Dunphy'll show you what to do. Mostly you're just there to provide an extra set of eyes. You know how to use a camera, right?"

Well the sarcasm was a little uncalled for. "Of course I can."

"Then you're good to go." Hunter held up a set of keys. "Here," he said, tossing them to Sean, who caught them in one hand.

She looked up at Sean questioningly, caught the twinkle in his eyes and hoped it was because he was happy about spending more time alone with her, even if it was for work. "Well, guess it's back down to the parking lot for us, then you can show me the ropes."

His eyes darkened, heated. "Looking forward to it, sweetness."

And with that loaded answer he went and pulled the door open for her, leaving her off-kilter and a little breathless.

CHAPTER FIVE

Learning the ropes, as it turned out, wasn't as daunting or exciting as she'd first imagined. And the flirting she'd been enjoying so much with him was gone now that Sean was in full recon mode.

Zahra stayed down low in the passenger seat as Sean checked the text message one of the other guys had just sent him. She cradled the high-powered camera in her lap, index finger waiting on top of the shutter button in case the suspect ever came out of his freaking building for her to get a shot of him. So far only a mother and toddler and an old man in one of those motorized chairs had come out.

"How long have we been sitting here?" she asked irritably.

"Not quite ninety minutes. Why, you getting bored or something?" he asked dryly.

Bored was an understatement, even for her, who thought staying in and watching movies alone on a Friday night was a good time. "This guy might not even be home, for all we know. Shouldn't we be doing something else? Helping the others follow their suspect maybe?" It seemed like such a gigantic waste of time for them to be sitting out here like this, doing nothing. She would've been far more productive back at the office working on translations or breaking encryptions for Alex.

She heard the smile in his voice when he answered. "Nope. Learning to be patient is the hardest part about surveillance work but it's also the most important. Just be glad you're all snug and cozy in this vehicle instead of out in the mountains lying in the snow right now with a pair of binoculars and a minus twenty wind chill."

She glanced over at him, curious. "Did you have to do that often?"

As he hadn't shaved in a few days his face was covered in dark stubble that made him appear rugged and dangerous. On him that look was sexy as hell. "Often enough."

"How long did you have to wait out there?"

He shrugged. "Sometimes for days."

Good God, she couldn't imagine anyone wanting to do that for a living. Suppressing a shudder, she kept her eyes trained on the front entry of the apartment building across the street from where they were parked. "You guys are insane."

"Damn straight," he said with such obvious pride that she couldn't help but smile.

In the lull that followed she mentally reviewed everything that had happened in the past week, and all the things left unresolved. "Think they're going to be able to find the mole?" she asked finally. It weighed heavy on her mind to think that someone within the agency—maybe even someone she knew—was handing information about them to the TTP and the domestic sleeper cell here in Baltimore.

"Sooner or later, yeah. I'm hoping for sooner though. That bomb almost killed Gage, and it could've been any, or all of us."

She'd seen at the time that Gage being injured had affected him, she just hadn't realized how much until he'd told her last night about the friends he'd lost in the line of duty. When he'd walked into the office to tell her about Gage, he'd been so upset she'd instantly been compelled to get up and hug him, letting her guard down in that moment to comfort him. That first taste of being held in his strong arms had haunted her ever since. It was addictive and she wanted more, wanted to be the center of his focus as he touched her and studied her reaction to every stroke of his fingers, every caress of his tongue on her body.

His gaze shifted back to the building and he tensed slightly. "Someone's coming out. Keep your head down."

Zahra swiveled, aimed the camera toward the front door and waited, making sure her face was hidden and the lens didn't show, as Sean had taught her. Through the telephoto lens she had a clear view of the building's front entry. A man appeared in the foyer. Around her age, mid twenties or so, dark hair and golden skin.

"He's got a full beard, well groomed," she reported. The shots she'd seen of him previously all showed him with a very short goatee.

"Could still be him. Take some shots so we can compare them later with the facial recognition software."

The man pushed the door open and emerged into the bright afternoon sunlight wearing shades. Zahra took several frames in quick succession, the shutter making a quiet little click with each shot. "Is it him?" she asked. Bahir Sahota had been flagged by the CIA as possibly linked to the terror network her NSA team was trying to nail.

"Think so. Make sure you get his profile as well."

She waited for him to walk down to the sidewalk and turn up the street before taking more of him from the side. As he walked away from her and got into a silver compact car, she sat forward to zoom in on the license plate and snapped a few pictures of it. Sean waited until the silver vehicle was halfway up the street before he started up the SUV and followed.

Zahra stayed quiet while they tailed him out of the urban neighborhood and headed west toward the city center. Sean didn't talk as he drove, focused on staying close enough to the vehicle to follow, but far enough away to maintain their cover. The driver exited off the highway and took the turnoff to the city center. Staying on him now was harder and she marveled at the skill Sean showed in maneuvering through heavy traffic while keeping the target vehicle in sight.

They lost the silver car at a red light. Calm and decisive, Sean wound his way through two lanes of traffic and cut over the next block in time to catch up with it.

"You're good," she told him. "I don't think he has any clue he's being tailed."

"He won't if I do my job right," he answered, switching lanes again. "And you didn't."

She blinked. "I didn't what?"

"Know you were being tailed."

"You tailed me? When?" Other than last night.

"Last week when you met Claire and her friend for dinner. Gage sent me to keep any eye on you guys. I sat in the parking lot the whole time, waited while you talked out on the sidewalk, then followed Claire home to make sure no one else did."

Since she had no idea what she was supposed to say to that she didn't respond and made a mental note to be more vigilant about what was going on around her from now on. What else hadn't she noticed? After the attack she'd been paranoid about people even looking at her but it had faded after a while because she'd started to feel safe again. Apparently over time she'd gotten too complacent and let her guard down too far. Sean had just given her a very pointed reminder about how vulnerable she was.

"Well, this is interesting," Sean commented a minute later when the silver car turned onto a road lined with apartment buildings.

"Why, what's going on?" she asked, watching as the car parallel parked at the curb and the driver climbed out.

"Hang on a sec," Sean said, then got on the radio to Hunter. "I'm sitting in front of the building you guys were watching yesterday," he told him. "We've followed a guy here—we're ninety-five percent sure it's Bahir—and he's up at the front door right now. Zahra, he's got something in his hand. See if you can get a shot of it."

How could he see that from here? She scrambled to get the camera up in position, managed to snap a few frames as Bahir stood at the front door. "It looks like an envelope," she said. "Too thin to have a stack of money in it. Whatever it is, it's thin."

"He's alone?" Hunter asked, a note of urgency in his voice.

"That's affirm. Whoever he's looking for isn't home. He tried the buzzer but no one's answered," Sean said.

"The suspect we were tracking yesterday," Hunter answered. "Has to be. They attended the same mosque."

Zahra's muscles tightened as the connection hit home. She kept her finger on the shutter button, her heart pounding. "Which mosque?" she asked, afraid she already knew the answer.

When Hunter said the name her fingers froze around the camera, her blood turning ice cold. She must have made a sound because Sean set a hand on her forearm. "Hey, what is it?"

She swallowed and shook her head, fighting the nausea twisting in her gut. "I used to go to that mosque." And so had the man who had taken everything from her.

Sean cursed and keyed the radio again. "Hunt, someone just let him in. A woman, standing in the foyer. Stand by."

Surfacing from the dark wave of fear tugging at her, Zahra blinked and refocused on the building's entrance. Bahir was gone but reappeared a moment later without the envelope and walked back to his car.

"He's heading back to his vehicle," Sean reported to Hunter, "but the envelope's gone. He must've dropped it in someone's mailbox."

"Amir," Hunter confirmed, voice hard.

"Want me to follow this guy now? See where he goes from here?"

"Negative, I'll bet my left nut he's just a delivery boy. Get back to the office and make sure you run the photos Zahra took. We'll meet you there, and once we know for sure you saw Bahir, we have to find this Amir asshole and figure out what he's up to."

"Roger that." Setting the radio down, he turned to her and reached for her hand. "Jesus, you're freezing. What the hell's wrong, Zahra?" When she shook her head he caught her chin in one hand and tilted her face up, forcing her to meet his eyes. "Talk to me." He brushed his thumb gently across the line of her jaw. His gaze was so sincere, so concerned.

Though she wanted to lean into his hand and blurt out everything, she just couldn't. The memories were too raw, too shameful.

Instead she laced her cold fingers through his and squeezed, grateful for his warmth and that he seemed to genuinely care about her. "Just get me back so we can work on the pictures," she told him. "I need to talk to Alex." He was the only one who would understand.

Eyes burning with frustration and disappointment, Sean gave a grudging nod and kept hold of her hand as he started the ignition.

Amir spread his feet and arms apart for the guard to pat him down and turned when he was told to so the officer could check the back of him. The air in here was still and smelled of stale sweat. The weak fluorescent lights overhead bathed the room in a sickly, depressing wash of bluish light. His pulse beat an erratic rhythm just from being inside these walls, his mind whispering he'd wind up in an even darker place than this if he wasn't extremely careful.

The fake passport and Social Security number he carried named him as an approved visitor from the mosque that matched the list the prison had on file. Even though his beard was bushy enough to conceal most of his lower face and he planned to shave it off tomorrow to help disguise his appearance again, he knew he was being monitored on camera right now and that his sudden appearance might raise red flags.

"All right, go ahead," the guard ordered gruffly and waved him through the electronically locking door into the next room. Dozens of other visitors sat at tables waiting for an inmate to be escorted from the cell block. Young women with children—who the hell would bring children in here?—other family members and friends of the incarcerated, some church group volunteers.

Making his way to the front of the room where the inmates were separated from the outside world by thick sheets of Plexiglas, he told the guard who he was here to see and chose a seat at the window. He sank into the hard orange plastic chair attached to the wall by a thick steel pipe and rubbed his damp palms over his jeans. People behind and beside him spoke in hushed tones, the gray and sterile atmosphere pressing in on him.

A few minutes passed before a guard appeared with a new prisoner. Amir's heart rate quickened when the inmate came into view wearing a bright orange jumpsuit and a white *topi* prayer cap. The man's gaze traveled along the line of windows, stopping when it landed on Amir. A flare of recognition lit those dark eyes, the only sign that he recognized Amir.

He watched the man approach the seat on the opposite side of the glass, his ankles shackled and his hands bound before him with chains, shoulders drooped. He lowered himself slowly into the chair and Amir was shocked at the change in the man's appearance. It was as though he'd aged a decade in just two years. The thick head of dark hair and beard he remembered were heavily streaked with gray. His face held a sickly pallor, the skin sagging on the bones from all the weight he'd lost since his incarceration.

Amir reached over to pick up the black phone receiver hanging on the wall and waited for the man to do the same before speaking. "Ibrahim, peace be upon you," he said in Urdu. "It's been a long time."

"And upon you, peace," Ibrahim replied, his eyes wary. "A very long time, yes. What brings you here? I haven't had a visitor from the mosque since right after they locked me up in this hole."

Amir hid a wince at that and struggled to hold the bitter gaze boring into him. His skin crawled at the thought of being caged in here, locked away from the rest of the world to spend the rest of his days slowly rotting in a cell. "A friend asked me to come see you. He needs your help with something." He had to be extremely careful with his wording because not only were they being watched; their every word was being recorded. Though anyone overhearing him likely wouldn't speak Urdu, all it would take was the effort to find a translator and then they'd be after him too.

Ibrahim studied him intently before replying. "And what is that?"

"I'm looking for..." He mouthed the name *Zahra*.

The older man's eyes flared and he sucked in a harsh breath. His whole demeanor changed, the tired, defeated posture vanishing as he straightened and leaned forward. "Why?" The word was hoarse, throbbing with emotion.

"Do you know where she is?"

"No." His eyes were burning, the coiled energy seething in him palpable through the glass. At least Amir had learned what he'd come here to determine. Ibrahim might not know how to locate Zahra, but he was willing and eager to assist. Though there wasn't much he could do from behind bars, perhaps he could provide useful background information later on if they needed it.

"Do you know how I could find her? She's in danger."

A mute shake of his head, then his expression turned speculative. "You know something."

Amir nodded. "My friend called me a few hours ago. He found out she's been invited to a function tomorrow night. I'm going to see if she shows up, so I can warn her." Hopefully his lie would go unnoticed if anyone translated the conversation later.

Ibrahim searched his eyes, seemed to hold his breath for a moment. "What are you going to do?"

"Me? Nothing." Then he smiled. *I'm going to carry out Allah's will and finish what you started, brother.*

CHAPTER SIX

The drive back to headquarters was tense. A brittle silence lay between him and Zahra and he didn't know how to ease her. She was still visibly shaken by the news about the men on surveillance, her lips pressed into a thin line and her arms wrapped around her waist in an attempt at self comfort. He'd give anything to have her open up and let him soothe her but she'd completely shut him out. His temper did a slow burn all the way back to the office and up the elevator. By the time they hit the sixth floor, it had spilled over into a simmer and the silence was grating on his nerves like the scrape of sharp fingernails over a blackboard.

When they finally arrived on their floor and stepped out into the hallway, Sean knew she was going to walk away and couldn't take it anymore. He snagged Zahra's arm with one hand. She stopped and looked up at him in surprise and he quickly tugged her into an empty office and shut the door.

The instant the mechanism clicked she yanked her arm from his grasp and turned to face him with a belligerent expression. "What?"

Seriously? Sean fought back his annoyance, tried to keep his tone calm when he felt like shouting at her. "Tell me what happened back there. You know something, and whatever it is it scared the hell out of you, so just tell me. Let me help." It drove him crazy that she was afraid and wouldn't let him do anything about it.

The anger in her face faded, replaced by a weary sadness that made him desperate to wipe it away. He'd seen that look often enough over the years to understand what it meant. He'd seen it in soldiers who'd watched their teammates die in a firefight and in helpless civilians caught in the crossfire and witnessed their entire family being wiped out in a single misplaced airstrike. He hated seeing that same haunted look in Zahra's eyes because it told him she'd suffered some unspeakable trauma in the past.

"I told you, the men we're tracking are affiliated with the mosque I used to attend," she said.

"Yeah, and about that. I had no idea you were a practicing Muslim, let alone religious at all." She didn't wear a headscarf and he'd never seen or heard anything about her praying the required five times a day, so to say the mosque thing had surprised him would be an understatement.

Zahra wrapped her arms around herself and held his stare. "I'm not anymore. Not since I left for college when I was eighteen."

Christ, it was like trying to pry a locked vault open with nothing but his bare hands. "Do you know those men?"

"No."

"Is it possible they know you?"

"It's possible they know *of* me," she answered cautiously.

What the hell was that supposed to mean? He dragged a hand through his hair, wanting to shake her. Why wouldn't she trust him with this? "That's it? That's all you're gonna give me?"

She huffed out an exasperated breath, appearing equally frustrated that he wouldn't let the matter drop. "Look, I was raised in a really strict traditional Muslim home, all right? Traditional to the point that I attended mosque every Friday and prayed five times every day and wore my headscarf as all good and modest Muslim girls should. I was raised with the expectation that once I graduated from high school I should allow my father to find me a suitable husband and stay home to raise all the babies we had together. Over time the restrictions became much worse. I watched my beautiful religion become twisted right before my eyes and start to destroy my life."

"Your father did that?" Zahra was cautious and somewhat conservative, but she was a proud and modern westernized woman in every way. Given what she'd just told him, that must not have gone over well at home. Had her father beaten her whenever she'd done something to defy his authority and establish her independence? All Sean's protective instincts flared to sudden, violent life. He remembered the remark she'd made to him at the safe house last week when she and Claire had served them lunch. *Don't get used to it. Just because I'm a brown girl doesn't mean I like running around serving you guys food.*

That comment suddenly held a wealth of new meaning.

Zahra nodded, her expression resigned, tired. "He hated that I refused to follow the traditional role he insisted God wanted for me," she explained with a shrug. "It was my mother who secretly encouraged me to follow my dreams and study hard while I was growing up. When I won an entrance scholarship to MIT in my senior year of high school, you bet your ass I took it and got the hell out of there as soon as I could. I left everything behind to start fresh, including my mother, who sacrificed *everything* to give me my freedom. And I left her there in that suffocating prison of a home, Sean. I. Left. Her." Her voice hitched and he felt like someone had punched him in the gut when he saw the sheen of tears glistening in her beautiful eyes. "When I tried to make it right the year I graduated, I..." She trailed off, shaking her head as she stared at the floor.

Her mother, Sean realized with a sudden jolt. She'd told him last night that her mother had died. Had she killed herself? Waited until her daughter was safely out of the house before she found the only way out she could?

He reached for her, opened his mouth to comfort her but she held up a hand to ward him off and gave a sharp shake of her head. "I hate everything about radical Islam, and that's why Alex recruited me. He knows how motivated I am. Working here gives me the chance to make up for what I did wrong in the past. I'm going to help snuff out Islamic terrorism every chance I get."

For a moment Sean was too stunned by her speech to reply. Alex had recruited her? Holy shit, even knowing that little bit of her past he had even more respect for her and what she'd made of herself.

Holding her defiant gaze, he found his voice. "I believe you, and I'm proud as hell that you've fought for what you wanted, what you believe in." He chose his next words with care. How could he say what he was feeling without making her feel weak, which was the last thing he saw her as? She was a fighter and he loved that about her. "I just want to be here for you, make sure you're safe."

He caught the flare of shock that flickered in her eyes and wasn't sure if she was surprised by what he'd said or if it was the idea that anyone would want to do that for her. Either way, it twisted his heart until a fierce ache filled his chest.

"Thank you," she acknowledged with a nod, her voice just above a whisper. "That means more to me than I can say."

Then let me in. Trust me to take care of you. He wanted that so much it shook him. And while he wanted to wrap his arms around her and hold her close, physically express how much he cared about her, he forced himself to remain still and swallow the hundred additional questions crowding his throat. If he pushed her now he knew she'd shut down, maybe for good. He wasn't willing to risk breaking the tenuous bond of trust they'd established. "You can count on me. You know that, right?"

A tremulous smile quivered on her lips, as though his words had touched her deeply. God, did she feel that alone? It was killing him not to touch her. "Yes, I do trust you, and that's why I wanted you to go with me tomorrow night. In light of all this I'm not sure if I'm still going, but I'll let you know, okay? I just really need to talk to Alex right now."

The man who'd recruited her after whatever tragedy she'd experienced. Sean found that point very interesting.

Recognizing that the conversation was over and that he wouldn't find out anything more from Zahra, Sean relented with a nod and opened the door for her. Zahra walked quickly down the carpeted hallway and waved to Ruth, who was at her desk. "How did your interview go?" she asked her.

Ruth lowered her gaze, looking tired and drawn. "Fine. Just glad it's over."

Zahra reached out to rub her shoulder in silent support then lowered her hand. "Is he free now? I really need to see him."

Ruth met her gaze questioningly then nodded. "Go ahead and wait for him in his office. He should be nearly finished by now. I'll have him come straight up when he's done."

"Thanks." Zahra strode for Alex's office at the end of the hall, pausing there to look back at Sean over her shoulder. "I'll see you later."

Since there was nothing to say at that point he nodded and turned left to head to the conference room. Hunter and Ellis came in shortly thereafter and together they reviewed all the new intel with Evers, the FBI agent attached to their task force. About an hour later the door opened and Sean looked up as Gage walked in with Claire.

Hunter smiled and stood to shake his second-in-command's hand, whose bright blue eyes were still bruised underneath from the explosion. "Hey, man, good to see you."

"It's good to be back," the red-headed former SF master sergeant replied. "Hearing's not a hundred percent yet, so y'all make sure to talk loud if you want me to hear you."

"Sure thing, old man," Hunter teased.

"Heard that, you fucker." In his early forties, Gage was still in prime physical condition despite his recent brush with death and his skills in the field were sharp as ever.

Hunter reached for Claire and pulled her into a hug. "Hey, gorgeous, how are you?"

"Much better." Cute and curvy with shoulder length light brown hair and gray eyes, she was a computer genius and one of the only people he'd seen Zahra hang out with socially. She eased back and acknowledged the rest of them with a smile. "So, how's the investigation coming along?"

"Got some interesting leads to follow up on, so it'll be great to have more hands on deck," Sean said.

"Yeah, but mostly I'm just happy to see Gage because I've missed his cooking in the worst way while you guys were gone. Dunphy almost killed us the other night. Spiked our food with a bottle of weapons grade ghost pepper hot sauce," Ellis put in.

"Guilty," Sean admitted.

Gage's blue gaze landed on him, a twinkle of admiration there. "That so?" he asked in his North Carolina drawl. "Well,

I'm glad you boys missed me because I'm itching to get back to work."

Claire shook her head as she rounded the table to sit next to Sean, muttering something under her breath about stubborn-ass alpha males. "All right, bring me up to speed," she said to him.

Sean showed her what they'd uncovered in her absence and Hunter coordinated the team's activities for the next twenty four hours. He and Gage divvied up and doled out more recon assignments for them, Sean and Ellis. This Amir guy, whoever he was, was in a world of hurt once they locked onto him.

On his way to the parking lot, Sean stopped at Alex's office and knocked on the door.

"Come in."

He found Alex alone, at his desk, and shut the door behind him.

Alex looked over at him, away from the document he'd been reading. "What's up?"

Rather than sit in one of the chairs opposite the desk, Sean leaned a shoulder against the door and folded his arms across his chest. "Where's Zahra?" She hadn't come back into the conference room after her meeting.

Alex didn't bat an eyelash. "Working. What else can I do for you?"

"You can tell me what's going on with her, what happened to her after she left for college and how she got that limp."

"Can't do that."

Sean reined in his temper with effort. Unloading on the boss was never a good idea and losing his cool would have no effect on a seasoned SF operator like Alex anyway. Still, he couldn't let it go. "I saw the look on her face when Hunter confirmed those two assholes attended the same mosque she used to. She went pale and now she's talking about not going to the awards ceremony tomorrow night. Is she under direct threat?" Aside from the FBI and CIA, if there was any chatter or new intelligence about an imminent attack within the NSA, Alex would know about it.

The older man shook his head. "There's nothing that would suggest she's being targeted specifically, no. And the only mention of her being involved in the dinner is one instance in yesterday's paper so it's doubtful anyone looking for her would even notice. Just her name and affiliation with MIT was in the article, nothing connecting her to the NSA, and nothing confirming that she was actually attending. I talked with her about it and she's decided she still wants to go as long as she has protection there. You're still going with her, right?"

Sean snorted. "Damn right." Over his dead body was she going anywhere unescorted right now. He did feel a little better that Alex didn't seem concerned that she was in danger though. The man might be a hard-ass agency guy now but there was no way he'd put any of his people in harm's way without warning them first. "What about the interviews? Any leads so far?"

Alex shook his head and leaned back in his chair with a sigh. "Everything we've checked out so far has hit a dead end. We've interviewed the most likely suspects already but we've still got a ways to go. Lot of people to go through here, you know?"

Yeah, Sean did know, and he also knew it was unlikely they'd uncover the mole before the cell tried to act. That kind of intensive investigation running records and everything else on this scale would take time. "One other thing about Zahra. Last night when I showed up to her place she panicked when she saw me holding my SIG. Did someone hold her at gunpoint? Was she shot?" Because those were the only reasons he could think of for such a strong, instinctive reaction to merely seeing a firearm. He thought of her limp, felt sick with helpless rage at the thought of someone deliberately harming her, let alone at the visual of a bullet tearing into her vulnerable flesh.

Something moved in Alex's eyes but it was gone too quickly for Sean to figure out what it was. "You know I can't discuss her personal details. Let me just say that she had a tough upbringing and then went through hell. Most people in her position would never have recovered from what she went through. Yet Zahra did. I know this award means more to her than she'll ever admit to anyone, and I think it's important that she goes to this dinner to receive it. She's earned it and I want her to have that recognition for herself. She placed her confidence in me when I recruited her long before the interview process and I can't betray that, so if she opens up about the rest to you in time, that's her call, not mine. But the fact that she's willing to attend this thing tomorrow night is because you'll be with her. That should tell you everything you need to know for now."

Sean mulled all that over before responding. "All right." He couldn't deny that it filled him with a fierce pride to realize that Zahra did trust him, maybe more than anyone, except Alex.

"She's a good girl who deserves a hell of a lot better than what life's dished out to her so far." A smile softened Alex's face, made those pale eyes less frigid and Sean could see how fond he was of Zahra. "All the shit going on here right now has dredged up a lot of baggage for her. I'd consider it a personal favor it you'd make sure she enjoys herself tomorrow night."

Sean knew Alex could tell he had strong feelings for her, and he seemed to approve of that. He relaxed his stance. Show her a good time? He'd love nothing more. "I will."

Amir was only three hours into his eight hour shift when he got the call to contact his handler from the designated safe zone. It took him off guard because they would only get in touch with him if something important had happened. Since he had no passengers at the moment he immediately made his way to a highway on-ramp and drove out to BWI. When he was safely in position of the dead zone he called the number he'd been given.

The same contact as the first time answered in Urdu and got straight to the point. "We've confirmed the op for tomorrow night."

A surge of excitement rushed through him. "Where?"

"Zahra Gill will be attending the Baltimore Four Seasons event at seven o'clock tomorrow evening."

"Are you sure? The last I heard it was only a possibility."

"We have verified this morning that she has confirmed she'll be attending."

"Alone?" He couldn't believe that someone so smart would be so stupid in light of recent events.

"Perhaps, though it's likely she may have someone else accompany her. Her RSVP was marked for two people."

"A bodyguard?"

"We don't know, but it doesn't matter. Do you have a plan in place?"

He'd been toying with a few ideas but if she had someone with her it would be more difficult to isolate her. If her guest was actually a trained bodyguard—possibly one of the

Titanium Security members—then this assignment had just become very dangerous indeed. "I'll be ready. Do you have any other instructions?"

"Just that if any other members of the team are with her, take them out too."

"I will."

"Malik is growing very impatient with the situation. He wants the targets taken out immediately, no more waiting. We're handing you this assignment on a silver platter. You understand what will happen if you fail tomorrow night?"

Amir's grip tightened on the steering wheel. "I'll complete this mission," he said forcefully, trying to ignore the spurt of fear that shot through his veins. Malik Hassani was a merciless taskmaster. People who crossed or failed him had a way of disappearing and winding up dead, or suffering such unspeakable torture that they wished they were dead. Amir knew he was locked in now. By agreeing to take on this assignment he'd also bartered his life in the process.

"Contact us as soon as it's taken care of."

"I will." Because if, Allah forbid, he botched the job tomorrow night, he knew he'd never be able to run fast or far enough to escape Hassani's reach, even from half a world away.

CHAPTER SEVEN

Sean released Zahra's elbow and put a guiding hand low on her back as they entered the crowded Four Seasons ballroom. His palm settled against the small of her back and the feel of the warm, firm flesh beneath that silky black dress sent the blood rushing to his groin. At the touch she glanced up at him through her lashes with those hazel green eyes and gave him a smile that was far too sweet for what he'd been thinking about on the drive here.

Things like what she had on underneath that dress, what her skin would feel like beneath his hands if he peeled that clingy fabric away, the way she'd taste and the sounds she'd make if he pushed her legs apart and put his mouth to her.

Sean forced his eyes away from the tempting glimpse of cleavage he could see from his taller vantage point that allowed him to look down into the bodice of her dress, and swept his gaze around the room. Much as he wanted to keep staring at her, he was here to ensure she was safe and enjoyed herself. He'd make sure of both.

He barely noticed the hitch in her stride as they headed for their table near the windows overlooking the inner harbor, and doubted anyone else would either. Especially if they were male. No red-blooded man in the room would be noticing her gait right now. They'd be too focused on her shapely ass and flat stomach once they peeled their eyes off the enticing curve of her breasts.

Noticing several men checking her out, he tightened his hand against her lower back possessively. The knee length gown she wore covered her entire back yet even with its modest neckline, on her it still managed to be sexy. She wore her long black hair twisted up in a sleek coil with a few loose tendrils framing her heart-shaped face that softened her angular features. The delicate scent of her perfume trailed up to tease him. He wanted to take her some place private and press her against a wall as he fisted his hands in her hair and ate her up.

Oblivious of his thoughts, she glanced up at him with those clear eyes and gave a wry smile. "I guess I have to stop being an introvert for a while until dinner's served, huh?"

"Probably a good idea." If she was nervous about coming here she hid it well. Other than the way she kept glancing around the room, she gave no outward sign that anything was worrying her. Nothing had tripped his inner radar on the way here and while he'd continue to keep an eye on what was happening in the room, it was time to enact the next phase of this operation.

He slid his hand around her waist and squeezed, noting the subtle way she stiffened. "One thing, though."

"What?" She tilted her head back to see his face, her tone holding a note of suspicion.

"Just to keep our story straight, how long have we been dating?"

She blinked at him in surprise. "Does it matter?"

"Yeah, it matters. I want to make it convincing. Are we new, with lots of sparks? Or are we long haulers and well into our comfort zones?"

A hint of amusement sparkled in her eyes, and he suddenly very much wanted to hear her laugh. Really laugh. "Very new. Lots of sparks."

Fine by him, and not a hardship acting the part with her. Sparks it was.

She eased away from his hold and put a discreet distance between them. "Should we mingle now?"

"By all means." He snagged her hand and threaded his fingers through hers, charmed when she shot him an uncertain glance. If that little public gesture was enough to rattle her, he couldn't wait to see how she'd react when he started turning up the heat. Maybe he hadn't been looking forward to sitting through this dinner initially, but things were about to get interesting. This evening was going to be memorable, that was for sure.

He accompanied her to their table while she introduced herself, admiring her poise and how easily she was able to engage strangers in conversation despite being outside of her comfort zone. This kind of forced, stuffy socializing was something he'd never been good at either, but he could handle it for a few hours. He would put his true talents to use soon enough, he thought, hiding a smile as he pictured what her reaction would be.

He stayed right beside her through all the handshaking and required social graces. In between scanning the room for possible threats he answered direct questions from several people but didn't say any more than he had to. After a couple times, people left him out of the conversation altogether, which was better because then he could do his job more easily.

When he heard her stomach growl during a lull in the conversation, Sean took it as their cue for a break. She'd been working at the office with Claire all day and he knew what a workhorse she was so he doubted she'd eaten for hours. She was probably starving. He slid his arm around her waist, hugging her into his side. "Let's get you something to eat, sweetness."

Zahra looked up at him in surprise at the endearment, but didn't argue.

He made himself smile at the group around the table, though it probably didn't look very friendly. "Excuse us." Without another word he pulled her away toward a waiter with a silver tray full of appetizers.

"I'm not really very hungry," she protested.

"Yeah you are. You're just too nervous to realize it."

She frowned at him. "I'm not nervous."

Sure you're not. He snagged a couple napkins from the waiter and examined the tray. "Do you like spanakopita?"

"It's okay," she answered distractedly, glancing around the room.

"You don't need to keep doing that," he said, low enough that only she could hear him. "I promise you I've got it covered. Everything's fine."

When she looked back at him he brought the bite-sized piece of stuffed phyllo dough to her mouth.

Her eyes widened and her lips parted slightly in surprise. He took advantage of the opportunity to slide the pastry between her lips. When she tentatively accepted the morsel and tried to pull her head back, he followed with his hand, forcing her to close her lips around his index finger. Her cheeks turned a pretty shade of pink, but she didn't protest, accepting the bite and sucking gently as he withdrew.

The soft parting stroke of her tongue against his fingertip sent a rush of blood to his groin. His dick pressed painfully against his zipper as he watched her chew. Shit. Now all he could think about was seeing that mouth wrapped around him while she knelt before him and he tangled his hands in that thick, shiny black hair to hold her in place.

She chewed for a moment, a slight frown wrinkling her forehead as she swallowed. "What are you doing?" she whispered.

Getting way too fucking turned on. "Taking care of you. My instructions were to make sure you're safe, happy and well fed. I intend to fulfill my duty."

"I can feed myself, thanks." Her lashes dropped as she lowered her gaze to his chest and reached for the rest of the appetizers he held.

He pulled the napkin out of reach. "Now what fun would that be?"

Her eyes flicked up to his, full of wariness.

"Want another one?" he asked.

She considered him a moment. "I think maybe you misunderstood what the arrangement was supposed to be."

He lifted another bite of spanakopita and offered it to her. "I don't think so. You wanted sparks. Let's make some."

She held his stare for a moment, her resolve clear. "Fine. As long as you know it's for show."

"Absolutely." That didn't mean he couldn't enjoy the hell out of seducing her for the next few hours. "Now be a good girl and let me feed you." He brought the flaky pastry to her lips, brushing gently against that tempting lower curve and took pleasure in the way her eyes darkened with sudden sexual awareness before she masked it. *Too late, sweetheart*, he thought with a smile. She appeared cool and reserved on the surface, but he knew better and was willing to bet she was a powder keg inside.

Those cool green-tinted eyes stared up into his defiantly as she accepted the bite of food. Sean smothered a grin and fed her a few more mouthfuls. She might be annoyed right now, but she couldn't deny she felt better with something in her stomach. And she definitely wasn't looking over her shoulder anymore. She was too busy staring holes in him. As long as she wasn't worried anymore, he didn't mind. He for damned sure liked distracting her this way.

"I've had enough," she said when he reached for another piece. "Aren't you going to eat?"

"If you feed me."

An impish smile on her lips, she accepted the challenge and took another pastry from a passing tray then lifted it toward him. Sean caught her wrist and held it, staring straight into her eyes as he bent his head and gently, slowly closed his mouth around the morsel in her fingers. Her quiet intake of breath, the way her pupils expanded, made his heart pound. Keeping hold of her delicate wrist, he licked the flakes of pastry from her skin before releasing her.

She was staring at his mouth now as if she couldn't look away, her hand frozen in his grip. That delectable flush was spreading down her throat to her upper chest and Sean was dying to see if she'd turn that color all over beneath his hands and mouth.

As though coming out of a trance, she blinked and withdrew her hand, dropping her gaze as she took a slow breath. "Okay, I think that's enough sparks for the evening."

Oh, not even close, sweetness.

She grabbed a napkin and wiped her hands, still avoiding his gaze. Flustered and aroused and so beautiful it made him ache. "They're going to serve dinner soon."

"Okay. I'll let you go, then." His eyes snagged on a tray of chocolate dipped fruit sitting on the table beside them. "Right after you have one last treat."

Deep in the shadows of the Four Seasons parking lot, Amir shut off the ignition and tugged the brim of his hat down lower on his forehead. He'd shaved off his beard and put on his reading glasses for good measure but it drove him nuts that he had to sit out here in plain view of anyone who passed by until the dinner was over. Even he wasn't brave enough to storm into the ballroom and start shooting. He had decided on this one course of action and now he had to follow through with it, even if things were far more complicated now.

Zahra definitely had a bodyguard with her. One of those Titanium guys, though from his earlier vantage point he couldn't tell if it was Hunter Phillips or Sean Dunphy when the man had escorted her through the front lobby doors a few minutes ago. Not that it mattered whether it was Phillips or Dunphy; they both had elite military training and if Amir wasn't extremely careful tonight he might not survive the operation. He also hadn't seen where they'd parked or what vehicle they'd arrived in. Had they taken a cab, or had someone dropped them off maybe?

His heart rate was elevated and his palms damp as he watched other hotel guests come and go. The sky was turning from purple to blue and the overhead lights around the lot cast long shadows everywhere. Cries from the seagulls near the water's edge sounded faintly over the roar of his pulse in his ears. His fully loaded pistol lay tucked beneath his seat. He'd already checked it three times, no sense in doing it again no matter how nervous he was being in this stolen pickup for the next hour or two. This spot gave him the ideal view of the front entrance and hopefully he'd be able to see which vehicle they got into once they left the hotel. With all the people around he couldn't afford to kill them here.

But once they came out and he spotted their vehicle, their minutes left on earth were numbered. His best chance was killing them before they got mobile. Exhaling a ragged breath, he scrubbed a hand over his face and settled in for the agonizing wait.

Why was he doing this to her?

Zahra held back a sigh as she watched Sean select a ripe red berry from the tray. The grinding in her stomach had lessened, so she was thankful he'd insisted she eat something. His method, however, was turning her on to the point that she could hardly breathe. It was hard enough for her to be here with all these eyes on her, but having to maintain her vigilance while playing along with Sean was proving too much for her. She didn't like being taunted with what she couldn't have. She knew that as soon as the task force was finished Sean would leave. Flings might have been her thing in the past, but not now, and never with him.

For what felt like the hundredth time she questioned the wisdom of coming tonight. Talking with Alex had allayed her fears but all she really wanted was to get through this and go home, change into her comfy robe and cuddle up in bed with a book for awhile. Maybe if all went well tonight she'd be able to sleep all the way through without waking up soaked in sweat and her heart pounding in her ears.

When he turned back to her, Sean's dark eyes glittered with an erotic heat that stole her breath. He stood close enough that she had to tip her head back to look into his face, and held up a chocolate covered strawberry to dangle it in front of her mouth. "Open up, sweetness."

Combined with the sexual awareness in his eyes, that deeply intimate tone sent a flare of heat into the pit of her stomach and between her thighs. Held prisoner by his intense gaze, she parted her lips as he placed the berry against them. And he didn't stop the seductive move there. Instead of popping the morsel into her mouth, he eased it partway between her teeth and held it there, watching her closely as she bit down and sucked the juices away so they didn't spill down her chin. Sean flashed a predatory smile and bent his head, stopping only when his warm breath feathered over the corner of her mouth.

"Wider."

The erotic whisper made her grow slick and swollen as she envisioned another naughty scenario. Him holding his erect cock out to her like he was offering a treat, one hand gently pulling her head close enough for him to brush the slick head against her waiting lips. She shivered, struggled to concentrate.

As though he knew what she was thinking, he smiled and pressed the berry more firmly against her parted lips. "Come on, sweetness, open wide. I know you want it."

God, did she. The suggestive way he said it made her go liquid. Licking her lips, she parted her mouth and allowed him to slide the berry in. She bit down, taking the rest of the fruit up to the stem, closing her hand around his strong wrist to hold him still. Meeting his stare, she boldly slid her tongue out to stroke across his thumb and fingertip, then closed her lips around them and gave a slow, firm suck.

Take that, she challenged him silently.

The amusement in his eyes vanished, replaced by white hot desire. His gaze narrowed on her mouth, so full of heat it practically singed her face. When she released his hand and lifted her head, she wasn't the only one breathing faster.

Sean reached up to glide his thumb across her lower lip, his expression absorbed. "Dinner," he managed in a rough voice, then grabbed her hand and took her back to their table. She barely remembered what they ate or what everyone talked about during the meal. She sat through the speeches and awards without being able to concentrate, constantly distracted by the feel of Sean's thigh pressing against hers or the feel of his fingers stroking over her bare shoulder when he draped an arm across the back of her chair. She shifted and pressed her thighs together to stem the throb there but it didn't help. God, she wanted him so much it hurt.

When the man at the podium called her name Sean rose to pull out her chair and help her up. She smiled at him in gratitude, knowing he'd done it not only as a courtesy, but to spare her any embarrassment her stiff hip might cause her in front of an audience as she got to her feet.

Pulling in a deep breath she made her way across the room to the podium and accepted the award, aware of Sean's eyes on her the whole time. Her entire body tingled and her heart raced with a mixture of excitement and pride. The award represented far more than recognition. It was a physical representation of everything she'd fought for, and would continue to fight for.

A lump formed in her throat as she accepted the plaque and headed back to her seat. Her mother wasn't here to see this but Sean was and that warmed her to the soles of her feet. He was waiting for her when she reached their table. His proud smile touched every part of her heart and when he slid a hand behind her nape and pressed a lingering kiss against her forehead right in front of everyone she feared she might start crying.

The rest of the evening passed in a blur and finally it was over and she could be alone with him. It had been a long time since she'd been interested enough and had the guts to ask a man back to her place, but for him she was willing to put aside her fears. Even if tonight was all they had together, she wanted to do it. Needed to. Her body was on fire and he was the only one who could douse the flames.

Sean laced his fingers through hers and raised her hand to his lips to kiss the back of it on the way down to the lobby. Zahra pressed closer to his side and breathed in his clean scent, every nerve in her body humming with desire. She noticed him carefully scanning the lobby on the way through but even the reminder that they might be in danger didn't dampen her arousal.

All the way through the lobby he kept her off to the side of the room, blocking her subtly with his body while they waited inside for the valet to bring their SUV around to the side exit, rather than the front where they'd be more exposed. By the time they were outside at the SUV where the valet had left it in a secluded spot that afforded them concealment and protection, she couldn't wait another second to touch him. She dumped her plaque and purse on the ground and set her hands on his broad shoulders, her fingers pressing into the muscle beneath the tuxedo jacket. She tipped her head back to stare up into his eyes.

Sean gazed down at her with such hunger that she shivered and when he slid his hands into her hair she couldn't control the soft sound of need that slipped out of her. His eyes darkened and he leaned in. Zahra rose up on tiptoe, expecting him to crush his mouth to hers, and let out a startled moan when he instead pressed his face against the side of her neck and inhaled deeply. Goose bumps flashed over her skin, pebbling her nipples until they chafed against the lacy fabric of her bra. Her fingers tightened on him and she closed her eyes when she felt his lips rub against her neck, the soft caress a stark contrast to the whiskers on his face.

"Zahra," he breathed against her skin, nuzzling her with his nose and lips. "You're so damn beautiful."

"God, just kiss me," she demanded, grabbing fistfuls of his hair to force his head up. People were walking past them just yards away and she didn't even care so long as he didn't stop what he was doing to her.

Sean resisted at first, instead opening his mouth against the sensitive place beneath her ear to let his tongue drag against her skin. She gasped and tugged harder and then he at last turned his head and kissed her. But he didn't shove his tongue inside and fuck her with it as all the other guys she'd kissed had done. No, Sean seduced her with the glide and shifting pressure of his lips against hers. His hands held her still when she tried to take more, making her wait, building the need higher. When she whimpered in frustration and pressed her body against his to ease the ache in her breasts, he finally licked his way into her mouth.

Zahra squeezed her eyes shut at the exquisite feel of him. He tasted like the crème brulee they'd eaten for dessert and he took the time to caress every sensitive spot in her mouth with velvet soft strokes of his tongue. She quivered and melted, responding to the languorous caresses with a desperation she couldn't control. By the time he lifted his head to breathe she was trembling all over, a mass of shivering need.

He seemed much more in control than she was. His gaze was tender and hungry on hers as he trailed his fingers across her hot cheek, the hard bulge of his erection lodged against her belly. He shifted his thigh until it pressed between her legs, his eyes flaring when she whimpered and rubbed against him, delirious with sensation. "I want inside you."

"Yes," she blurted, lifting her head for another kiss. Anything he wanted, she'd give him, as long as he took the terrible ache away.

Sean growled low against her lips and took her mouth more aggressively this time, though he continued to tease her with those sinful caresses of his tongue that turned her liquid in his arms. She'd never been kissed like this, like she was the most desirable woman on earth and he wanted to keep doing it all night. If he took that same approach while they were actually having sex, she didn't know if she'd survive it. It had been so long and he made her forget all her inhibitions, all her fears about enjoying the pleasure her body craved.

She was ready to climb his body to find some relief when he tore his mouth away and buried his face into the curve of her throat. They were both panting. He released her hair and slid his arms around her back for a tight hug, then eased away and pressed her into the open doorway. "Get in."

Still drunk on him, she did as he said, scooping up her purse and plaque from the ground. She fumbled for her seatbelt when he closed her door and came around to slide behind the wheel. She drank in the sight of his profile, hardly able to believe she was going to have him naked and all over her the moment they got to her place.

He shook his head as he steered through the parking lot, the muscles in his jaw clenching. "If you keep looking at me like that I don't know if I'll be able to wait until I get you home to peel that dress off you and make you come against my tongue."

Zahra sucked in a breath and pressed her thighs together, desire slicing through her so deep she felt dizzy. The swollen bundle of nerves at the top of her sex throbbed as images of his dark head between her legs flitted through her brain. Her skin was hypersensitive all over, her silky dress and underwear suddenly chafing her skin. For one crazy moment she contemplated stripping naked for him right there in the front seat to see what he'd do, then thought better of it. She wanted to savor every moment of what was coming, in the privacy of her own bed.

To distract them both she reached out and switched on the stereo. Eddie Van Halen's guitar riffs filled the air and the knife-sharp tension in the vehicle dissipated. She kept her hands folded in her lap, not wanting to distract him as he drove, knowing he was keeping an eye out in case anyone was trying to follow them. She looked over at him in surprise when he took her left hand in his and set it atop the console separating their seats. Smiling to herself, she relished the simple gesture and the gentle stroke of his thumb. The anticipation added an edgy sort of sweetness to the whole thing. Having to wait would only make it better once it finally happened and she could hardly bear it.

They didn't speak, only Sean's beloved Van Halen breaking the silence for them as he drove toward her place. She was so focused on the fantasy images of the two of them naked in her bed, savoring the little caresses he bestowed on the back of her hand, that she didn't notice the change in him at first. Realizing that he'd just taken a third turn in a row and his thumb had stopped moving, she glanced at him. Immediately she noted the change in his posture, the stillness of him as he focused on something in the rear view mirror.

Suddenly chilled, Zahra tightened her fingers around his. "What's wrong?" She knew something was wrong and the first flutters of fear curled in her belly.

A muscle twitched in his lean jaw and his hand shot out to kill the radio, plunging them into immediate, jarring silence. "We're being followed," he said, and pressed harder on the accelerator, speeding along the darkened, almost deserted road.

CHAPTER EIGHT

Sean had noticed the silver Ford pickup behind them about a mile from the hotel. After watching it stay in the rearview mirror on the highway, he'd taken an exit and turned onto a side street to see if they had a shadow.

Since this was the fourth turn he'd made into a quiet residential neighborhood and that pickup had just turned onto the same street, he knew this was no mere coincidence. He picked up the radio and contacted Hunter. "We've got company."

"Where are you?"

Sean relayed their current position. Their best bet was to lose their shadow on the highway. Get on, dodge through the lanes of traffic and duck onto an exit before they could follow.

"Copy," Hunter said. "We'll get in the truck and head your way. Keep me updated."

"Roger that." He made another left turn and hit the gas. The sound of the engine revving filled the otherwise silent interior. He didn't have to look at Zahra to know she was afraid. "Everything's gonna be okay," he told her. "Just sit back and make sure your seatbelt is locked tight." He didn't waste time explaining that he had advanced defensive driving training because he doubted it would make her feel any better. She jerked on the strap and sat rigid in her seat.

Keeping most of his focus on the road, he glanced back at their tail every few seconds. The driver had given up all pretense of caution now and was getting closer in the mirror. Sean was already doing well over eighty in a forty zone, so whoever it was, they were flying.

There were no other cars on this stretch of road. He knew the general vicinity where they were but didn't know any of the streets. Up ahead the next traffic light was a stale red. He kept his foot on the accelerator as they approached, saw a car pull to a stop on the other side and then one drove through the intersection. Their tail kept coming, showed no signs of slowing at all. He pressed down harder on the gas pedal, counting on the light to change by the time they got there.

Zahra grabbed the edge of her seat and cried out. "Sean!"

Ignoring her, focused on getting them as far away from that silver pickup as fast as possible, he headed straight for the intersection. At the last moment the light changed. He flew through it at well over double the speed limit and didn't let up. Checking in the mirror he saw the truck fly through a late yellow light. "Hang on," he said grimly. He had to get them off this road and back on the highway.

Waiting until the last possible moment, he hit the brakes and cranked the wheel hard right. The tires screeched as the back end swung out. Zahra cried out and gripped the dashboard with one hand. "Just close your eyes while I get us out of here," he suggested, bringing the vehicle back under control to hit the gas again. A flashing red light down the street signaled a four-way stop. This section of town was more crowded; he couldn't maintain this speed without serious risk of killing someone in a collision.

The pickup was only a block behind them. He jammed on the brakes and took a sharp left, cursing under his breath when he had to bring them to a plunging stop to keep from plowing into the back of a minivan.

Zahra sucked in a breath. "Sean—"

"Just close your eyes," he snapped, and jerked the wheel to weave around the slower vehicle. The street was filled with parked cars, increasing the danger that he might hit someone if they didn't see him coming and stepped out onto the road. Silently raging at himself for picking the wrong goddamn escape route, he wound his way through the traffic amidst blasts of horns from pissed off drivers, narrowly avoiding another two collisions before he finally managed to get them onto a clear street.

The screech of tires and more horns alerted him that the truck was still coming even before it turned the corner. Sean was already making a hard right at the next intersection when the headlights appeared in the rearview mirror. Having the advantage for the moment and knowing they'd hit an on-ramp sooner or later on this road, he raced on. Only a few oncoming cars passed them and the next light was way off in the distance. The lights behind him disappeared suddenly. Startled, Sean didn't ease up on the gas just in case.

"Is it gone?" Zahra asked shakily, turning in her seat to check.

"Dunno, and I'm not taking the chance that it's not." Up ahead he could finally see the big green sign that marked the on-ramp, stating it was just a quarter mile up the road. The sooner he got them on the highway, the sooner he could get her to safety.

Zahra faced forward again. "Where are we going now?"

The on-ramp was dead ahead. Only a few more seconds. "We'll meet up with Hunter once I get us clear. I want to make sure we can verify that your place is still secure." He started to take his foot off the accelerator.

The pickup shot out of a side street ahead of them, directly in their path.

"Shit!" He hammered the brakes and wrenched the wheel to the left. The SUV swung around sharply in a controlled skid. Zahra cried out and grabbed hold of the dash to steady herself but as he righted the vehicle he heard her head smack into the window. He didn't have time to see if she was okay because the truck had caught up to them during the one-eighty. Sean's head snapped backward when the car smashed into the left rear quarter panel. Metal crunched. He heard Zahra's frightened cry as the impact forced them toward the shoulder.

Swearing, Sean floored it. He caught the muzzle flash then the sharp thud of bullets hitting the side of the SUV. Another smashed into the left passenger window, putting a spider web pattern into the bullet resistant glass.

Automatically he reached over and grabbed the back of Zahra's head, pushed. "Get down!"

Two more rounds hit his window. Zahra screamed his name and he released her head to grab the wheel with both hands. The truck rammed their left side again. The force of it spun the back end around and sent them careening toward the center line. Another car was coming at them in the opposite direction. On instinct he hit the brakes and shifted to neutral to turn them completely. It didn't help. The pickup's bumper had locked with the SUV's and the added weight made the turn impossible. The combined momentum carried them across the center line and toward the trees lining the far shoulder.

He barely had time to yell "Brace!" before more shots peppered the SUV.

Motherfucker. Despite the superior weight of the SUV Sean could do nothing but try to control the skid, couldn't even release the wheel to grab for his own weapon and return fire.

In his peripheral vision he saw Zahra's arms flail out to grab the dash as those trees raced toward them. The tires squealed and smoked from him locking up the brakes in a last ditch effort to slow their speed. They shot off the road and slammed into the trees head on. His airbag punched him in the face as his seatbelt snapped taut. He grunted as it jolted hard against his ribs.

Disoriented, scrambling to get his bearings, his only thought was to protect Zahra. He looked over to find her shoving at the airbag, gasping in short bursts. As he reached over to release her seatbelt, more shots exploded against Zahra's window. She screamed again and ducked down just as Sean hit the release button, sending her to her knees on the floorboard.

He darted a glance over to see that the impact had wrenched the truck free from the SUV's bumper. The asshole was now less than twenty yards away, taking pot shots at them. "Stay down and don't move," Sean ordered Zahra. Livid, running on pure adrenaline, he reached into his shoulder holster for his SIG as he muscled his damaged door open. It finally gave with a grating squeal of metal on metal and he scrambled around it to use the engine block as a shield. This bastard wasn't using armor piercing rounds but he wasn't taking any chances by making himself a bigger target. He heard the sound of the pickup's engine revving as if the driver was planning to ram them again.

Rising to peer over the hood, Sean gripped the pistol and fired three precise shots through the driver's side of the windshield. The rounds plowed through the glass and the revving stopped. He crept cautiously around toward the end of the hood for a better angle. Damn, with the glare of the headlights he couldn't tell if he'd hit the bastard or not. He raised his weapon to fire again. Dirt sprayed up from beneath the Ford's tires as it swerved suddenly and fishtailed back onto the pavement.

This idiot thought he could drive a truck shot up like that? "No you fucking *don't*," Sean growled and ran out from behind cover to fire again. Two more bullets hit the back window but all he saw was the shape of a head ducking down as the truck roared away, out of range. It lurched around the corner and disappeared from view.

Heart racing, furious that he'd nearly gotten Zahra killed and the shooter was getting away, he lowered the pistol and got pissed off all over again when he realized he hadn't even gotten the complete plate number. Swearing at himself, he shoved the weapon back into the shoulder holster. A few oncoming cars had noticed the SUV and were slowing down to help. One driver rolled his window down, eyed him and the bullet-riddled vehicle cautiously.

"You okay, buddy?"

"Yeah. Call 911, would you?" Sean called back. He needed to get Zahra out of the SUV and someplace safe before that son of a bitch came back for more. He was only vaguely aware of the aches and pains in his body as he reached for the passenger door handle. The front end had only some crumpling because of the armor plating but the rest of the frame had sustained some damage as well. He had to set a foot against the body and use all his leverage to haul Zahra's door open. The dome light came on to illuminate her.

She was huddled on the floor in a ball, didn't look at him as he knelt down and reached for her. Because of the bullet resistant glass the windows were still intact so he wasn't worried about her being cut up from bits of glass. The impact from the crash and the airbag concerned him though. "Hey, it's over. He's gone," he said, pushing her hair away from her face so he could see her. Her eyes were squeezed shut and she was rigid all over. A tiny cut over one eyebrow seeped blood sluggishly, probably from the airbag. He swept it away with his thumb.

"Zahra," he tried again. "Are you hurt?"

She didn't answer, merely sat there and shook, seemed to be struggling to breathe.

Cursing, Sean took her face in his hands, tipped her head up gently. "Honey, I need you to talk to me. Are you *hurt* anywhere? I don't want to move you if you're hurt."

No response other than her pulling away and curling up tighter, those taut gasps coming from her.

Sean pursed his lips. Other than the cut over her eye he didn't see any blood and she was moving her neck okay, so it was probably safe to move her. If the driver behind him had called for help it could still be a while before the cops and fire crew showed up, and he doubted the shooter would come back with a crowd around. He still planned to be vigilant though.

He reached in and slid an arm beneath her thighs and another around her shoulders. "We're gonna sit here until backup arrives, okay? We're safer in here than we are outside." Thankfully she didn't fight him but she didn't try to help him either. She was frozen in his arms, almost catatonic, as though her body had shut down from the shock.

Worried, he left her in the SUV to accept a blanket from someone who'd come to help. Unwilling to talk to them about the shooting or accident, he said a curt thank you and returned to Zahra, wrapping the blanket around her shoulders. Her eyes were open now. She curled her fingers around the edges of the blanket and stared through the windshield, not even acknowledging his presence.

Leaving her there for the moment he found the radio lying beneath the dashboard. He gave Hunter their location and told him what had happened, then turned back to Zahra. Several people had gathered around the vehicle, asking questions, trying to help. Sean told them all to back away then swiveled in his seat to look at her.

In the glare of the parked cars' headlights her face was way too pale, her eyes glassy, pupils dilated. She continued to shudder, so hard he could actually hear her muscles vibrating. "Zahra. Hey, look at me, sweetness."

The endearment seemed to get through to her. She blinked and focused on him.

"That's my girl. Okay. Take a breath with me."

She did, the shaky inhalation painful to hear. Maybe something had happened to one of her lungs when they'd hit the tree?

"Good. A few more. Just slow everything down. You're okay and I won't let anything happen to you."

A few more ragged gasps as she struggled to obey.

The wail of sirens sounded in the distance. Now that the cops were arriving on scene Sean allowed himself to relax his guard just a little. He wrapped a hand around the back of her neck, stroked his thumb over the side. She blinked at him, pupils still way too small, the level of constriction telling him how far in shock she was. "Are you hurt?" he asked again, holding her gaze.

All he got was a slight shake of her head, but it was enough to ease him. He'd begun to worry about a head injury from either when her skull had hit the passenger window during that turn or the coup-countercoup during the actual crash.

"The police are almost here and Hunter's on his way. Gage'll be with him, and Ellis too. They'll make sure we're covered, okay? I'm gonna stay with you the whole time."

Her eyes darted up to him for a second then went back to staring through the windshield and still she didn't respond verbally. He could hear her teeth chattering from the force of the shudders tearing through her. Feeling helpless he squeezed her nape gently, hoping his touch and voice were getting through to her. When she swallowed convulsively and shuddered again Sean smoothed a lock of hair back from her cheek.

He understood that she'd be frightened after what had just happened but what he was seeing went well beyond that. Zahra wasn't scared, she was fucking terrified. And from the haunted look in her eyes he had a feeling she was seeing something far different than the fractured window before them.

Biting back a curse, he gathered her up in his lap to hold her as the patrol cars roared up.

CHAPTER NINE

It felt like her heart and lungs were caught in a vise. Eyes closed, Zahra huddled against Sean's chest and struggled to get herself under control. But against the backs of her lids all she saw was fire and blood and death. Her screams blended with her mother's as the flames licked over them.

God. She shuddered, swallowed the bile rising in her throat. The memories were so vivid she couldn't shake them. Even the approaching sirens reminded her of that terrible night. To live through it a second time…

She buried her face in Sean's throat and wound her arms around his sturdy neck, needing the feel of him to anchor her in the present. Needing that sensory input to block out the phantom burning sensation in the scars on her back, the long dead nerve endings there suddenly flaming to life.

Sean tightened his arms and set his chin on top of her head. "Okay, baby, you're all right."

The quiet, calm tone and the way he held her so protectively broke through the shock like a bullet shattering a pane of glass. She hitched in a breath and squeezed her eyes shut tighter as tears flooded her eyes. Sean made a low sound and murmured soft things against her hair but she didn't hear the words. In the background she was dimly aware that the police had arrived and that Sean had lowered his window. Car doors opened and shut, people crowded around them and started asking Sean questions. When he loosened his hold to shift her away from him she shook her head and clung, still afraid and wanting to avoid the humiliation of having all these witnesses see her lose it.

"Just give us a few minutes," Sean said and the men backed off. "I'm just going to take you over to the ambulance so they can check you out, okay?" he told her, then opened his door and lifted her into his arms.

She looped her arms around his neck and kept her eyes closed as he strode for the ambulance, the strobe lights flashing against her closed lids. He sat on something and spoke to the paramedics for a minute, stroking her hair until she forced herself to take a shaky breath and sit up. They were sitting on the vehicle's rear deck. She blinked against the bright light inside the ambulance and wiped at her eyes, avoiding Sean's gaze.

"Okay now?"

No. Not even close. She nodded without looking at him, managed to say, "Mmhmm." He squeezed her hand once in reassurance as she eased off his lap and pulled the blanket tighter around her body. The paramedics looked her over and she answered their questions with answers consisting of a word or two. The older of the two who seemed to be the more senior one told her she was suffering from shock and a bit of whiplash, both of which she already knew. She cast a glance around and saw Sean standing near the SUV talking to the police. They were going to want to question her as well but right now all she wanted was to be alone with Sean, somewhere safe. But where was safe anymore?

When the paramedics finished their exam they waved at a policeman standing nearby. He came over and began interviewing her about what had happened. Her answers were short, her words slurred by the way her jaw kept trembling. She was still cold all over, could hardly answer all these things without the memories crashing over her in a suffocating tide.

Apparently satisfied with her cooperation, the cop left to talk with his fellow officers. Zahra glanced over and found the other Titanium guys had arrived. Hunter, Gage and Ellis stood with Sean at the ruined vehicle as he talked. Taking a bracing breath, Zahra held the blanket closed against her chest with one hand and set her palm on the ambulance floor to ease off the rear deck. The muscles in her right hip screamed in protest the moment she set her weight down on her leg. She gritted her teeth as the painful spasms gripped her limb, becoming aware of the aches and twinges in the muscles across her neck and shoulders. They'd hit that tree so hard, it was a wonder she hadn't blacked out.

Struggling to keep her balance, she walked unsteadily toward the men. Sean was having an intense discussion with Hunter, his back to her. Gage saw her out of the corner of his eye and headed straight for her before anyone else noticed her. Embarrassed by what the others would no doubt see as weakness, she was nonetheless grateful when he came over and wrapped a thick arm around her waist.

"You look a little shaken up still, darlin'," he said as he let her lean her weight on him and helped her toward the others.

"A little, yeah," she answered, glad he'd let her walk instead of carrying her.

Sean met them halfway, his eyes full of concern as they tracked over her face. "You hurt your hip again?"

She nodded, bit back a grimace as the muscles grabbed again. "Hit it against the door, I think. It's not too bad." Not as bad as the terror gripping her.

"C'mere," he said, taking her from Gage's hold. The moment he touched her and she got a whiff of his familiar masculine scent, tears pricked her eyes again. She blinked and focused on keeping her steps small as they went over to join the others.

"Can we go home now?" she whispered.

"We'll get you out of here ASAP, but I'm not sure we can let you go back to your place now. Gage has offered to let us go to his place instead. Would you like to see Claire right now?"

"Yes. Just get me out of here." She couldn't look at the SUV a moment longer without wanting to retch. The sight of those bullet holes and the memory of the crash brought too many nightmares back.

"Guys, let's get moving," he called out.

Hunter walked up and put a hand on the side of her face to get her attention. Startled, she blinked up into his light brown eyes, taken aback by the mixture of intensity and concern she saw there. In that moment she glimpsed another side of him she'd never seen before and understood what his girlfriend, Khalia, must see inside this hardened soldier.

He studied her for a long moment, those eyes searching hers. Then he nodded in satisfaction. "Thatta girl. You hang tough and we'll take care of everything else."

Blinking, Zahra could only nod at him in reply. He dropped his hand and headed for one of the two Titanium vehicles parked along the shoulder. Sean helped her toward it, keeping his strides small to match hers. Ellis opened the rear passenger door for them when they got there. He set a hand on her shoulder and squeezed gently then stepped back. Sean boosted her onto the leather seat and slid in beside her. "Normally we'd have to go down to the station and file an official report but Alex managed to pull some strings for us so we can skip all that," he told her.

"I'll have to remember to thank him for that later," she said.

Hunter got behind the wheel and started the engine. Assuming Gage and Ellis were in the other vehicle, Zahra reached for her seatbelt but Sean pulled her right into his lap and wrapped his arms around her. She relaxed against him and closed her eyes with a sigh, absorbing his strength and the heat his body emitted.

"I've already contacted Alex," Hunter said from up front. "He knows we're going to Gage and Claire's. We'll figure out what to do next once we get there. The cops and FBI already have teams out looking for the driver. Shouldn't be long before we know something."

Surrounded by quiet, Zahra was lulled by Sean's warmth and the gentle stroke of his hand over her hair. Suddenly her head snapped up to look at him. "Did you get my plaque and my purse?"

His lips quirked. "Now I know you're feeling better. Ellis has 'em, and your shoes."

She leaned back and rested her head against his sturdy shoulder, not in the least embarrassed about the public display of affection in front of Hunter. Sean seemed to like holding her as much as she loved being in his arms, especially right now.

The rest of the drive passed in silence and Zahra looked out the window as they pulled up to a modest two-story house in an unfamiliar suburban neighborhood. The porch light was on and Claire opened the door when Zahra stepped onto the sidewalk out front with Sean's steadying hand on her waist. At the sight of her friend, Zahra bit her lip and swallowed back tears.

Claire rushed down the front steps and met her in the driveway with a solid hug. "I'm so glad you're okay," Claire whispered, pulling back to search her face. "Come on inside and we'll get you warmed up."

There were boxes everywhere in the hallway and kitchen but that wasn't a surprise since they'd just gotten into town a few days ago. Sean helped her to the sofa in the great room and sank down beside her. Claire appeared with a patchwork quilt to spread over her.

"Want some coffee or anything?"

"Do you have decaf?" Zahra asked. Last thing she needed was a jolt of caffeine to her stressed nervous system.

"I've got herbal tea. Sean?"

"Coffee, thanks."

Claire hurried into the kitchen to make the drinks. Sean rubbed the tops of her shoulders gently. "You're gonna be sore later. I'll get Claire to give you some ibuprofen or something. I've gotta go talk with the guys for a bit."

"Sure." Though she missed the feel of him next to her she understood they needed to plan their next move and she was completely comfortable in Claire's company. Her friend came back with a steaming mug of tea and two painkillers a few minutes later.

"I laced it with lots of honey, to help counteract the shock, but it's hot, so be careful."

Zahra thanked her and curled her legs up beneath her, wincing as her hip seized again.

Claire sat at the opposite end of the couch and pulled her knees up. "If you want to talk about it, I'm here. If you don't, that's okay too."

A knot formed in her throat. She trusted Claire, enough that she almost blurted out everything about the night her mother had died. The words were there, burning a hole inside her, needing an outlet. Something made her hold back. Claire had been through hell these past few weeks and Zahra refused to burden her with more. Besides, she had Sean and she'd tell him everything later when they were alone. At least, she hoped they'd eventually be alone later tonight.

"I was thinking about how much I wished we had nothing more to deal with right now than a good old fashioned girl talk."

Claire's eyebrows went up in surprise at the abrupt shift in conversation. "Hey, I'm all over that. Why, you got an update about the no-man-for-six-months-I'm-gonna-be-a-crazy-cat-lady-instead thing?"

She put the pills in her mouth and took a sip of hot tea to wash them down. The sweetness of the honey was pleasant on her tongue. "It's a bit too early to tell how things are going to go, but yeah, I've decided against the cats for the time being."

Claire smiled, her gray eyes full of understanding. She knew how private Zahra was and that opening up about her personal life wasn't easy for her, especially if it involved someone they were working with. Claire knew perfectly well Zahra meant Sean. "Well, I'm here if you ever decide you want to talk about that too, okay?"

"Okay. Thanks." She took another sip of tea and set it on a coaster on the coffee table, her attention catching on the sparkly new ring on Claire's finger. "Why don't you distract me for a bit with what you plan to do for your wedding?"

Clearly excited to talk about it, Claire outlined the details until Sean came in and stopped beside the sofa. "We're definitely not going back to your place tonight, so we can either stay here, at my place with the guys or go someplace else if you have a better suggestion in mind."

She loved that he said "we", telling her he had no intention of leaving her for at least tonight. But stay here? She glanced at Claire, who was watching her.

"You're welcome to stay with us tonight and for as long as you want. If you want," Claire added.

She appreciated the offer, but considering how Gage had been targeted previously and now Sean and Zahra tonight, it seemed safer to keep them in different locations. She wasn't sure how the driver had found them tonight, but suspected the mole must have gotten wind of her attending the ceremony. That certainly narrowed down the list of suspects substantially.

Not wanting to think about that any longer, she tried to think of someplace safe and private she could stay with Sean. An idea popped into her head. A place she'd loved spending time in once but hadn't had the guts to go back to since her mother died. "Does it have to be in the city?" she asked him.

"No. Might not be a bad idea to get out of town for a few days, actually. We could head out of state if you want. Why, do you have somewhere in mind?"

If he was with her, she could face the ghosts of her memories. It was remote enough to give them protection and with only a few neighbors around the lake they'd have all the privacy they wanted. "There's a cabin we could stay in."

"Come with me."

He took her by the hand and towed her into another room where Hunter, Gage and Ellis were having a conference call with someone on speaker phone.

"That still Alex?" Sean asked. Hunter nodded. "Alex, Zahra has a possible safe location in mind."

"Where?" he asked.

"The place out at Deep Creek Lake," Zahra answered. He knew exactly what she was talking about.

"You still have it?"

"It was willed to me but it's listed as belonging to a corporation I set up, so it's not under my name. There's no way anyone could track me there." Only one other person knew the location and since he was locked away from society, he wasn't a threat to her anymore. "I was thinking I could go there for a few days until the situation settles down."

"Not by yourself," Alex admonished. "At least one of the guys will have to go with you."

"I'll take her," Sean said. The others didn't react. "If Hunt can spare me for a few days."

"Sure," Hunter answered. "How remote is it up there? Will you still be able to access files and whatever?"

"There's Internet access, but it might be a little on the slow side," Zahra said.

"Dunphy, make sure you check in with Hunter once you get there so he can keep you up to speed on what's going on. In the meantime, the others are heading out to see if they can find this elusive Amir and figure out what the hell he's been up to."

"Roger that." Sean turned his attention to her. "Sure about this?"

Sure about spending time alone with him in a safe location where no one but the team could find them? "Yes."

Careful to keep pressure against the wounds in his upper arm, Amir took the stairs up to his third floor apartment. He was lucky that no one else saw him as he did because there was no way for him to disguise the blood soaking the shirt he'd wadded up to stem the bleeding where the bullet had hit him. His legs were weak and his free hand shook as he pressed down on the metal release lever and stumbled into the hallway.

It was a miracle he hadn't killed himself trying to get home. He'd ditched the bullet-riddled stolen Ford a few blocks away from where he'd left his cab and forced himself to make it there on foot despite the pain and shock. If he was lucky the cops wouldn't find the blood trail he'd left. Now he had to patch himself up and clean up his cab in case someone came looking for him.

Entering his darkened apartment, he shut the door and let himself lean against it for a moment. The burning throb in his arm made it hard to think. He wasn't sure if the bone was broken but he couldn't afford to go to the hospital. The staff would report the gunshot wound and the cops would be there to arrest him before he'd even been treated.

He flipped on the light and went to the bathroom, hissing as he pulled the soaked T-shirt away to inspect the entry and exit wounds. He supposed he should consider himself lucky that the bullet had gone clean through and missed his chest or head. Fumbling with the tap, he got the water running and gritted his teeth in preparation for what was coming. A strangled scream ripped from his throat when the water poured over the wounds, feeling like acid against his raw flesh. Gasping, gagging, he watched the water run reddish-pink in the bottom of the tub and swirl down the drain. The bleeding wasn't slowing.

Amir forced himself upright and searched in the medicine cabinet for some bandages. The wounds needed stitching. He'd never put a needle in human flesh before but he'd seen it done and had no choice now. It took him endless minutes to find a needle and thread, get it through the eye and tie a knot in it, especially since moving the hand of his wounded arm caused him more pain. Before pouring hydrogen peroxide on the open wound, he glanced up at his reflection in the mirror above the sink. His now clean-shaven face was ashen, a sickly gray color and beaded with cold sweat.

Lowering his gaze to his bloody upper arm, he brought up the threaded needle with his good hand and bit down hard. The needle pierced the skin around the larger exit wound and he swallowed hard before pulling the thread through and pushing the needle into the skin on the opposite side of the wound to make the first stitch. Pain swamped him, made his head swim and his gut churn, almost as bad as the horrible spine chilling fear that numbed his brain.

He couldn't believe he'd failed. It was only a matter of time before his handlers found out about the botched attempt and took other measures. Amir had to take some of his own before that happened, no matter how desperate they were.

First thing in the morning he was going to be back at the prison for help.

CHAPTER TEN

By eleven o'clock that morning Pakistan time, Malik knew the operation had failed. What he didn't know was where the hell his operative was.

With an impatient wave he dismissed one of his closest advisors, grinding his back teeth together while he waited for the door to close behind him. The instant it did Malik shot out his arm and swept the entire contents of his desk crashing to the floor.

Nothing was going right. He didn't have the location of the Titanium team members and all of them were still alive. Though he'd put more pressure on the mole this morning, there was no further information about the team's whereabouts. It was probable they'd all scrambled again after the shootout.

Malik shook his head, the anger burning through his veins like a wildfire. Missing this hit was the second humiliation he'd had to suffer in the past ten days. He didn't intend for there to be another.

In the soundproof office he paced back and forth across the thick Persian carpet. Not only had Amir failed to kill Zahra Gill and whoever had escorted her to that dinner last night, he'd also dropped off the face of the earth. Malik knew he wasn't dead because his men had already checked with law enforcement, the local hospitals and morgues. No one matching Amir's description had been brought in. The police had, however, found the bullet-strewn truck he'd been driving. From the bloodstains in it they knew he'd been wounded, though how badly no one could say.

Where was the bastard now? In hiding? He couldn't possibly be stupid enough to believe he could escape Malik. With one phone call, one single *phone call*, he could have him either killed or dumped straight into American hands. Part of him wanted to do it, to teach him a lesson and remind everyone who worked for him that he was not to be trifled with.

The other part knew Amir was one of a few operatives embedded in the States who might yet be able to pull this off.

Either way, it was time to bring other, more powerful measures into this scenario. He was going to send a message to the American authorities.

Stalking back to his desk, he bent to pick up the phone now lying on the floor and punched in a number. "Activate the others and call Amir." He might not be answering his phone at the moment but Malik knew he'd be monitoring his calls and messages. "Alert him that he is no longer working alone and if he does not contact me within the next six hours, he'll be handed over to the Americans." Even if Amir wanted to get revenge for that he'd never be able to leak Malik's current location because no one but his most trusted inner circle knew where it was. All four of those men were with him now and were all secretly watching each other twenty-four hours a day.

"Yes, sir," the man answered.

"One other thing." Malik paused to trace the wood inlay on the front of his desk as he gathered his thoughts. "I want them to take the device with them."

A pause filled the line for a moment, as though that had taken the man off guard. "Yes, sir, I'll tell them right away."

"Good." He hung up and started picking up the mess on his carpet. Amir might be missing but he'd surface soon enough. All they needed was a location and the hunt could begin anew, only this time with a secret weapon that would make his statement loud and clear.

Sean turned down the access road to Deep Creek Lake Park just as the sun came up after a tense but uneventful three hour, one hundred and eighty mile drive to the westernmost part of Maryland. They'd left Gage and Claire's just after three in the morning, and the long night coupled with the constant state of vigilance every time a vehicle appeared behind them had started to take its toll on him. His neck and shoulders ached from the crash and the long drive and more than anything he wanted to drop into a bed and sleep with Zahra beside him all night. She had to be just as sore and tired as he was.

"Take your next left," she directed from beside him in the passenger seat, "then the second right. The cabin will be on your left about a quarter mile up."

He followed her directions in the darkness, much more at ease now that they'd left the city far behind. During the drive he'd been extra cautious and hadn't spotted anyone tailing them. He was looking forward to spending some time alone with her here to decompress…and a lot of other things. Mostly involving them naked in bed together. The brush with death earlier had only amped his primal and possessive feelings toward her. He wanted to hold her bare body against his, imprint the feel and taste of her in his brain. He wanted to possess her until he was buried as deep as he could go inside her and listen to the broken cries she'd make as she came for him.

She'd already gotten under his skin to the point that he knew he couldn't walk away from her after his contract was up with the NSA. After that kiss he knew she wanted him, he just didn't know if it went beyond the physical for her or not. And the look of startled wonder in her eyes when he'd ended the kiss had tied him in knots. He was glad to know she'd never felt this way before either.

Tightening his grip on the wheel, he pushed away the sexy image of her in the throes of release and made the final turn. As he steered slowly down the unpaved road in the early morning light, Deep Creek Lake appeared through the trees on their left. The manmade lake was the largest body of freshwater in the state and the perfect temporary hideout because it was remote enough to provide them with added protection. He couldn't see anyone else finding them here without a direct invitation, not for the next few days at least.

Ahead, the outline of a cabin appeared off the road. "That it?"

"Yes. There's a little driveway off to the side you can park in."

Sean pulled in, getting his first look at her place. The small, one story building was constructed of timbers and surrounded by trees.

"I know it doesn't look like much but the inside's really comfortable. There's plumbing and electricity, a wood burning fireplace if we get cold. A full shower too, and a fridge and stove," Zahra said.

"Honey, to me that's like a five star hotel." And she didn't have to worry about getting cold. Not with him here to warm her.

He cut the engine and set a restraining hand on hers when she started to undo her seatbelt. "Stay put while I look around." When she nodded he got out and closed the door behind him. The woodsy scent of the air wafted around him on a cool breeze that ruffled the surface of the lake. Overhead the trees swayed gently, the slight creak of the branches mingling with the sound of birdsong. The wind was picking up, the approaching rain storm moving in from the coast. Mottled clouds blocked out most of the sky, allowing only occasional sparkles from the sun to ripple on the water. It was beautiful. Peaceful. Exactly what Zahra needed right now.

Sean did a quick circuit to get the lay of the land, noting the wooden dock jutting out into the water a few hundred yards to the north. A few other homes and cabins were scattered around this part of the lake, still far enough away that he and Zahra wouldn't be bothered by any neighbors during their stay. He checked the darkened cabin next, found both doors locked and all the windows undisturbed.

Satisfied everything was as it should be, he went back to the SUV and opened her door. He helped her stand and climb the steps, noting how much she favored her right hip. He'd have to do something about that once they were settled. On the front porch she fished for the key she'd left hidden in a nook behind one of the wooden rocking chairs on the front deck that overlooked the water. She unlocked the door and pushed it open with a groan of the hinges. A wave of slightly musty air hit him as she stepped inside and flipped on the light.

Instinctively Sean set an arm around her and stepped past her to check things out for himself. The small kitchen joined with a living room where a white mantel that looked like it had been cobbled together out of vintage corbels graced the far wall. A little TV sat in the corner opposite a sofa and coffee table. The whole place was decorated in bright jewel tones that spoke of a strong feminine touch.

"The bathroom's back there," Zahra said, gesturing down the short hallway. "Both bedrooms are beyond that."

Sean walked through and flipped on the hall light, his boots thudding softly on the wide plank wooden floors. The full bath looked recently renovated, sporting a sink and vanity and a fiberglass combination tub/shower. At the end of the hall he found the bedrooms, both boasting comfortable-looking double beds and thick floral comforters.

He turned back to face Zahra, still by the door. She had her arms wrapped around her waist and was looking around the kitchen/living room with a wistful look that made him realize how hard it had been for her to come here. Where he saw a cozy cabin built for two, she saw whatever ghosts haunted her past. "Why don't you sit down and relax for a bit while I unload our stuff?" he suggested.

"I've been sitting for over three hours already," she muttered, and limped into the kitchen to start opening cupboards. Sean caught glimpses of mismatched cups and dishes as she checked each one.

"Be back in a minute," he told her. With his leather jacket on, his shoulder harness was concealed. She obviously wasn't comfortable with guns and he didn't want to put his on display in front of her. He stripped off his jacket and the holster, tucking the weapons away in the large duffle he'd brought with him that contained even more firepower. Not that he thought he'd actually need it, but he'd rest easier out here having his rifle as well.

He carried in his duffle and the bag of clothes and toiletries Claire had packed for Zahra and set them in the room he thought must be Zahra's. If she wanted him to sleep in the other room he would, even though he'd hate doing it. Next he carried in the groceries he'd run out to buy before they left Gage and Claire's place, along with the ice filled cooler that held other items. He brought them into the kitchen and placed them on the butcher block counter. Zahra was standing by the stove, head bowed, hands balled into fists. He stepped up behind her and set a hand on her shoulder, finding the muscles rigid.

"You okay?" A stupid question since he could see for himself that she wasn't, but he didn't know what else to say and wanted to give her a chance to open up on her own.

She pulled in an unsteady breath before answering. "Been a long time since I've come up here."

"I'm guessing not since your mom died?" It was obvious from the decor and her reaction that her mother had stayed here and Zahra was thinking about her.

Zahra nodded, sucked in a breath as though she was on the verge of tears. Sean slid his arms around her from behind and pressed his front to her back, reminding her without words that she wasn't alone. She settled her arms over his, squeezed once. "I'm glad you're here with me. I don't think I could've done this by myself. Too many ghosts, you know?"

Sean was silent a moment before speaking. It was nearly seven in the morning, she'd been through something traumatic tonight and now she was facing whatever demons of her past hadn't yet been laid to rest. "I think you're done in. Want to just crash now?"

"No, I want to get everything put away first. I just need to get used to being here." She pushed away from him and started unpacking the groceries and Sean didn't try to stop her. As they put everything away the wind began to gust against the window panes. Soon the first drops of rain began to patter against the glass and roof.

Zahra went to her bedroom to get everything organized and Sean stayed back to give her some space. He'd spotted a cord of wood stacked against the side of the cabin so he went out and gathered what he needed to start a fire. Once he had it going he sank onto the couch and stared into the flames, wondering what his next move should be. His body wanted Zahra, naked and willing underneath him, but he also wanted answers. With no one else to overhear or interrupt them, this was the perfect time to ask her about all those secrets she kept locked away from the world.

She came out of the bathroom a while later wearing yoga pants and a long T-shirt Claire had loaned her, her hair damp from a shower. She'd left it down so that it spilled in a dark curtain down her back. Seeing him on the sofa, she stopped and leaned against the hallway wall, her expression unreadable. He waited, staying silent.

Finally she looked into the fire and spoke. "This was my mom's place."

Sean sat very still, noting the tense set to her shoulders and the way her brows drew together.

"She bought it years ago with some money her parents left her in their will. They were from Pakistan too. As was my father," she said in a flat tone.

Willing her to continue, he made a low sound that told her he was listening.

Zahra gazed around the room, seeming to take everything in as though it was the first time. "We were supposed to come here the night she died. We'd had it planned for weeks."

The muscles in his stomach contracted.

"My father controlled her as much as he did me, but when I left for college he lost his hold over me. I did the normal co-ed things, but my rebellion went a little deeper because I'd been sheltered beyond anything my classmates could ever have imagined. The moment I left home I stopped wearing my headscarf, I stopped praying then worshipping at all. At college I lived in residence and made friends, went to parties and even drank for the first time in my life." Her eyes shot to his. "I started dating, occasionally hooking up with guys at parties. I didn't much care about anything but feeling alive. My father got wind of what I was doing and insisted I come home so he could deal with my 'shameful' behavior. No way in hell I was doing that.

"One day near finals in my last year my mom called me to say things were getting really bad. He was threatening to come and drag me away from school. Apparently he and his buddies at the mosque felt I'd shamed myself and my family and he'd become even more of a hardliner. I knew he blamed my mother and that she was probably taking the brunt of his anger even though she wouldn't admit it. So I told her I'd come for her, to get her away from him. I would pick her up the night after I finished my exams while he was out with his mosque buddies and we would escape here." She shook her head, her smile bitter. "I know it sounds like an idiotic plan now, but this was the only place we could think of to go where he might not find us."

Sean's heart rate picked up, his mind already racing ahead to where this was leading.

Zahra stared back into the flames. "He knew she'd bought this place soon after they arrived in the States but he didn't know she'd been fixing it up. She came out here every weekend she could while I was away, to escape." Her voice caught and it was all he could do not to get up and grab her, hug her tight to somehow keep the pain at bay.

"Where is he now?" he asked quietly.

She turned her head. Her expression was so hard and cold it sent a wave of foreboding through him. "In prison, serving a life sentence for first degree and attempted murder. And I hope he rots in there."

CHAPTER ELEVEN

If Sean was shocked by her statement or the barely contained rage behind it, he hid it well. He didn't move or say anything, just watched her and gave her the space to continue if she wanted. Unable to bear his gaze any longer she turned away and scrubbed a hand over her face. Now that he knew the horrible truth, the rest of the details weren't as difficult to talk about. She'd told him this much; he deserved to know the rest as well.

"What did he do?" he asked quietly after a moment.

Even without looking at him she could feel his attention still focused on her. Exhaustion pulled at her but she needed to get this out in the open once and for all. She wanted Sean to understand what had made her into the woman she was today, scars and all. Actually, part of her was surprised he'd been this patient about finding out. With his computer skills and his penchant for detail, she'd half expected him to do his own digging long before now. It relieved her that he hadn't.

"He found out what we were up to, probably from one of his friends who had twisted him into a zealot," she began at last, gazing at the books and pretty things her mother had set into the shelves on either side of the mantel. "I picked my mom up that night and we'd barely left town before he caught up with us. I didn't see him, didn't even think to watch for him. Then all of a sudden, he was there."

The memories played before her eyes like a horror movie no matter how hard she tried to stop them. Tonight had brought them all back in vivid detail. "I caught sight of a car speeding up behind us on the highway out of town and that was the only warning I got. He rammed us from behind, sent us flying off the road. I didn't have time to do anything but try to keep us from hitting anyone else. He hit us again on the side, and we hit the shoulder and flipped over. The car rolled. I remember hearing my mother screaming and the sounds of shattering glass and crunching metal. When we stopped I was pinned upside down in my seat. My pelvis and right femur were broken, I couldn't move. Then he started shooting."

Sean hissed but she couldn't look at him if she wanted to finish this. "A fire started, I don't know whether from the crash or the bullets. My mother was hurt from the impact and the two bullets that hit her. The fire spread fast and I guess because of the bystanders we'd attracted he took off. I got my seatbelt off. Someone reached through the broken window and grabbed me by the arm, started dragging me through no matter how loud I screamed. Somehow they got me out but then it was too hot for them to go back for another rescue. My mother was on fire. I had to lie on the grass and listen to her burn to death." Zahra had wailed in agony and grief, wanting to die as well. She shuddered at the memory, the blood-curdling sound of her mother's screams she'd never be able to forget. That was the hardest part, knowing she'd died in such unspeakable pain.

"Christ, Zahra..."

Feeling raw and exposed, she flinched away from him when he got up and walked to her.

Strong arms wound around her middle to pull her back against his powerful body. "I'm sorry. And then tonight it was almost the same again."

She nodded. "Whoever it was, he wanted to make it like last time. He knew my background well."

"Twisted motherfuckers," he muttered against the back of her hair. "God, no wonder you were so deep in shock earlier."

Zahra closed her eyes and leaned back against him, savoring his strength and the protectiveness of his embrace. "Guess whoever it was didn't count on me having a former Recon Marine with me."

He grunted and held out his arms. "Come sit down with me so I can hold you."

Her heart flipped over at the need in his voice, wanting the security of his arms around her too. She followed him to the sofa and went into his arms. Sean stretched out on his back and pulled her on top of him. With her head resting on the solid wall of his chest she listened to the soothing beat of his heart while he ran one hand through her hair. The wind buffeted the cabin, rain pattering on the roof. It should have been cozy and relaxing but she was too deep in her head to enjoy it.

His hand slipped beneath her shirt to rub her lower back, then slid higher. She knew the moment when he felt the hard, swirled patch of skin that traveled over the right side of her ribs to between her shoulder blades. Doctors had performed skin grafts to cover the burn but the scarring was still bad. Still, Sean didn't seem to mind her imperfections. Though the nerve endings were dead there, she could tell from the way his hand moved against her shirt that he was still stroking the area. "Did they have to operate on your hip?"

She nodded. "Three surgeries. My pelvis is stable at least but I've got pins and plates and rods holding my right femur together. I did a ton of rehab to strengthen the muscles surrounding the joint but my hip will never be as strong as it was and it gets fatigued really easily."

"Most people wouldn't even notice your limp."

"You did."

"I'm not most people."

She smiled at that. No, he wasn't. "And thank God for that, or I wouldn't be alive right now."

He kissed the top of her head and didn't answer, as though uncomfortable with the praise. "What happened afterward?"

"They arrested my father when I was still in the ICU. I didn't see him until I had to appear at his sentencing. He'd pled guilty to avoid the death penalty but I still had to give my statement before the court. It was awful." She hadn't realized she'd tensed until she felt the pressure of Sean's arms around her back, squeezing her. "I made myself look at him even though the sight of him made me physically ill. He sat next to his lawyer glaring up at me with so much hatred it makes my skin crawl to think of it. He hated me and everything I stood for. And you know what? I hate him right back for what he took from me."

"I would too."

They lapsed into silence for awhile. Now that she'd told him everything she felt lighter inside. He didn't judge her or pity her for her decisions and their consequences. "I think it will always haunt me though. I can't stop blaming myself. Part of me will always wonder if I hadn't left home, if I'd had a better plan, maybe my mother would still be alive."

"And if she was, it'd be both of you serving life sentences in the life he made for you," Sean countered.

True. All her therapists had told her the same thing, that she shouldn't play the "what if" card because she was suffering from survivor guilt and PTSD. Having a diagnosis didn't change the way she felt and didn't make it any easier to bear. It didn't erase the image of her mother engulfed in flames, her arms flailing in a futile effort to escape the fire.

Zahra squeezed her eyes shut and took a calming breath. "I'm doing much better these days."

"I can't believe how tough you are, to overcome something like that, let alone be so functional right now." His tone held so much pride that it made her throat tighten.

She rubbed her hand gently over the right side of his chest and shoulder, mapping the contours of hard muscle with her palm. It might mean heartbreak for her later but there was no way she could keep her heart out of the equation now. "Why didn't you check up on my background before?" She knew he'd been curious about her.

"I asked Alex about you but of course that was a waste of my breath, and that's as far as I was willing to take things. I didn't want to break your trust by going behind your back to look into something you obviously didn't want anyone else to know about."

Tipping her head back, she met his eyes. "Thank you."

His smile was so gentle it squeezed her heart. "You're welcome. I was tempted a time or two though, not gonna lie."

With his skills, it wouldn't have taken much for him to find out everything. His thoughtfulness surprised and touched her. "I'm really glad you're here with me. My mom would be too. Pretty sure she'd have already fallen in love with you."

"What about her daughter?"

Startled, a little afraid to answer, she lowered her gaze and pressed her cheek back to his chest. For a moment she thought about deflecting the question, then decided against it. She'd just told him her darkest secrets. If she could trust him with those, then why did she feel so vulnerable admitting her feelings? "She's headed in that same direction."

Sean caught her head in one hand and tilted it back to look at her. "Good," he said, staring right into her eyes. "Because I'd hate to be the only one."

Taken off guard again, Zahra lifted up on her forearms to stare down at him. He was so impossibly sexy all sprawled out beneath her, looking totally out of place yet comfortable on the girly sofa. She lifted a hand and touched her fingers to his lips, stroked the soft skin. His eyes darkened. He caught her wrist and kissed her fingertips. Cupping the back of her head in one big hand, he pulled her down as he leaned up. The kiss was gentle, almost chaste compared to what he'd done to her earlier, but the emotion behind it shook her to the bone.

Pressed flush against him her body flared to sudden, desperate life. Her breasts tightened, the tips hard and sensitive, and a restless ache built between her thighs. She shifted to get closer, opening for the caress of his tongue and moaned a little when she felt him harden against her stomach. He answered by taking complete control of the kiss, stroking her tongue and the roof of her mouth as he rubbed his erection against her.

In moments she was breathless, her heart beating erratically. Her body craved skin to skin contact, the release he could give her. She sucked his tongue, eliciting a low groan from him and parted her thighs to rub just the right spot against his hard length. Pleasure speared through her, swirling hot and needy deep in her belly. A strong hand curved around to cradle her bottom, holding her firmly against his hips as he rocked up against her, teasing her with the promise of what he'd feel like inside her.

The empty ache between her legs took on a sharp edge, her inner muscles clenching around nothing. She wanted him in her, filling and stretching her, soothing that ache. He was so hard against her, rubbing over the damp, cloth-covered flesh. Zahra moaned into his mouth and let the sensations run through her while her heart pounded and her mind went blank. Sean guided her movements with one hand on her ass and the other wound into her hair, but let her set the pace. A tremor ripped through her as the pleasure swelled higher, pushing her into desperate need when suddenly an insistent buzzing broke through the sensual haze.

She raised her head, hoping she was hearing things.

Drawing back, Sean stared up at her with barely leashed desire, nostrils flared, pupils dilated. "Worst fucking timing," he grumbled and reluctantly let her go.

Zahra rolled off him to the side as he sat up and pulled his phone out of his pocket. She listened to him talk to whoever it was and decided it had to be Hunter. "No, she's doing fine," Sean said. A moment later he frowned. "You're breaking up. Hang on." He checked his phone then looked at her.

"Try the front porch," she told him.

He went out on the porch and closed the door behind him. Through the window she could hear his muted voice. Sitting up, she scrubbed a hand over her face. The conversation went on for a long time and Sean didn't come back in. She was beyond exhausted, so she decided to head to bed. Leaving the door open in invitation, she slipped beneath the covers and cuddled up, hoping he'd join her. Minutes later the fatigue and drumming of raindrops on the roof pulled her down into sleep's embrace.

Amir made sure he was at the gates long before prison visiting hours began. He was the first in line when the guards came to take the visitors through security. Keeping his wounded arm at his side and his hand in his coat pocket to keep it from moving, he approached the guardhouse. The exertion made him woozy and his skin broke out in a clammy sweat.

"Your name's not on the list today," the guard informed him curtly, scrutinizing his appearance as he compared it to the fake ID. Amir knew he looked like death with his face so pale and the shadows under his eyes. At least the bleeding had stopped, his crude stitches holding for the time being.

"It's not?" Amir tried to mask his fear, the sudden leap of his heart at the guard's pronouncement. Coming here was a huge risk yet he had no choice. He had to speak to Ibrahim immediately. "It should be. I came in to see him the other day."

"Then why do you need to see him again so soon?"

Because if I don't find out where his daughter is they're going to kill me. "He asked me to come today. I should be on the list. Is there someone you can check with?"

Looking all kinds of annoyed, the guard grunted and shooed him off to the side. "Wait here until we've processed everyone else. Then we'll see."

Having no choice, Amir sank onto a concrete bench and waited. His arm throbbed like a separate heart beat and his stomach lurched from the constant pain. At most he'd slept a total of two hours last night, mostly in snatches of a few minutes each. Each time his phone rang his heart had tried to pound its way through his chest. He hadn't dared answer it but he'd listened to the messages.

When he'd heard one of his handlers saying he was to link up with the others once he found the Titanium team members, he'd realized he was trapped and called back to confirm.

At least this way he had a chance to finish the job and win his freedom, rather than be shot down by someone from Hassani's network.

The guard finished checking everyone and motioned him over. Amir pushed to his feet and walked over, every step jarring the burning wound in his arm. Another guard joined the first one, both wearing latex gloves and ready to pat him down. Did that mean he was going in?

"We're gonna let you in this once because you're on his approved visitor list and because our computer's down so there's no way for us to verify whether you got your name on the list last night or not. But this is a one-time thing and won't happen again. You want to visit, you have to be on our list."

He almost closed his eyes in relief. "Thank you."

"What'd you do to your arm?" one asked him.

"Had a biopsy done yesterday. Skin cancer scare," he answered.

Apparently satisfied by the lie, they patted him down for weapons and contraband. "All right, go ahead."

With a silent prayer of thanks Amir entered the visitor's area and took a seat opposite the Plexiglas wall. It took a while but finally Ibrahim appeared. The moment he saw Amir his eyes lit up. He sat and took the receiver from the wall.

"Is it done?" he asked.

Amir wanted to squirm in his chair. "No. I...no."

The excited light in his eyes died. "What happened?"

"There was someone with her when I tried to warn her," he said slowly, careful to keep up the lie from last time. "A man. Very well trained." He nodded pointedly at his arm, shifted enough for Ibrahim to see the edge of the bandage he'd slapped over his hasty patch job.

"Then why are you here?" he asked disdainfully.

"I need your help to find her again."

"Mine? How can I help you from in here?" he said with a bitter laugh.

"I have to find her, within a day or two at most." At this point Zahra was still his best chance at tracking any of the team members.

"I can't help you." Those dark eyes were cold now, so cold Amir suppressed a shiver because he knew if Ibrahim had been on the outside, Amir would be sorry.

He blew out a frustrated breath, barely refraining from dropping the receiver and dragging a hand through his hair. "There must be something you can tell me that might help. Would she go to a friend's house? A relative's?"

Ibrahim shook his head. "She is many things, but not stupid enough to do that after last night. And I don't know who any of her friends are anyway."

Damn. "What about another city she has some connection in?"

Another head shake.

"A sport or hobby, something that I could find a trail that might lead me to her?" He knew he sounded desperate but he didn't care.

"No."

"A favorite place she might go?"

Ibrahim started to shake his head and the spark of hope burning in Amir's chest flickered out, leaving him cold and in the dark. Then the older man stilled and Amir saw a flare of something in his eyes as they stared at each other.

Anticipation. It made Ibrahim's dark eyes gleam and Amir's heart thudded hard against his ribs as he waited for him to speak.

"There is a cabin," he said at last.

CHAPTER TWELVE

Zahra awoke to the sound of a door creaking open. She blinked as her eyes adjusted to the light coming through her open door from the hallway. Gray, muted daylight peeked through the small window beside her bed. The wind had picked up while she'd been asleep. It moaned and gusted against the wooden exterior of the cabin, pattering it with pine needles and bits of branches. Rain pounded on the roof. She wasn't sure how long she'd been asleep but she stopped thinking altogether when Sean stepped out of the bathroom rubbing a towel over his hair. Her built, sexy bodyguard with those strong arms that had sheltered her so securely, kept her alive and safe tonight despite the risk to his own life. And he'd done it all without hesitation or asking anything in return.

She came up onto her elbows to face the door as Sean walked over and leaned against her bedroom doorframe, carelessly draping the towel over one broad shoulder. Backlit in the hallway, he stood unmoving with his arms crossed over his wide, bare chest. His incredibly hard, muscular chest she'd cuddled against earlier. She drank in the sight of him there in nothing but his jeans, noting the tribal bands tattooed around both his biceps. Never a fan of ink before now, she had to change her opinion on that at the mouth-watering sight before her. On him those tats were sexy beyond belief, framing the bulge of his muscles.

When she tore her eyes away from the sculpted expanse of his naked torso, her mouth suddenly went dry at the raw lust she read in his face. "Hi," she managed in a whisper, tucking a lock of hair behind her ear. She sat up and brought the blankets up to shield her breasts that tingled beneath his gaze, the T-shirt suddenly an inadequate cover. "Was I asleep long?"

"No, but sorry I woke you. Didn't think you'd be such a light sleeper."

She'd always been like that, but especially now. She was wound tight as a watch spring from the attack and also because she didn't have the guts to outright invite him into her bed. Her cowardice was a huge disappointment. What more did she need than another near death experience to teach her to live life to the fullest? He was right there in front of her and clearly interested. Why couldn't she just go after him? She licked her lips. "Did Hunter give you any new intel?"

He shook his head and when he didn't say anything else, nerves started to take hold. Why wasn't he making a move? Was he waiting for her to do it? Had he changed his mind?

She fiddled with the edge of the comforter, searching for something to say, battling against the rising need inside her. *Hold me. Make love to me so I can forget these terrible memories for a little while.*

He still hadn't moved from the doorway, just stood there watching her with that unreadable expression she couldn't decipher. "If you want to work some more I can get up and help," she offered. Her fingers worried the edge of the quilt faster. *You're such a chicken shit, Zahra. Tell him you want him.*

What the hell are you waiting for? "There's not much in the fridge, but maybe I can fix us something…" Her voice frayed and she swallowed the nervous lump in her throat, wondering if she sounded as dumb as she felt.

Sean unfolded his arms and prowled toward her.

Zahra held her breath as he crossed the room, her heart thudding against her breastbone. He strode to the edge of the bed and sat beside her hip, the mattress dipping under his weight. In the added light coming from the hallway she could see the way he searched her eyes for a moment. Then he reached up and cupped the side of her face with one hand. She almost closed her eyes in relief.

His palm was warm against her skin, his thumb gentle as it swept over her cheek. A jumble of emotions swamped her. Fear. Desire. Uncertainty. Loneliness. Need. A need she didn't fully understand, but wanted to explore with Sean. She trusted him implicitly.

Gathering her courage, Zahra brought one hand up and curled her fingers around his strong wrist. Her gaze dropped to his mouth, so soft and full on what were otherwise such hard, masculine features.

Without a word, Sean brought up his other hand to cradle her face between them and lowered his head to kiss her. Zahra moaned and slid her hands into his thick, damp hair, opening her mouth for the soft caress of his tongue. Bolts of heat swept into the pit of her stomach and between her thighs.

Strong hands pressed her shoulders back onto the bed. She went willingly and lay staring up at him in the dimness, trembling all over. Anticipation, nervousness and desire all swirled through her in a dizzying rush. The edgy need he'd woken in her earlier was back full force, making her entire body throb and she was more aware than ever of just the bedding and T-shirt covering her. But part of her still balked about doing this. On some level—because of the strict way she was raised—she still felt intrinsically guilty about engaging in premarital sex. Whenever she'd taken a lover in the past, the sex hadn't lived up to her expectations at all. She was a little afraid of disappointing Sean because all the guys had made her feel like her inability to reach orgasm with them was her fault.

But she'd also never been this turned on before, and that was all Sean's doing. She wanted this. Hell, as a grown, healthy woman with natural desires, she *deserved* this. And she knew instinctively she wouldn't be disappointed this time.

As though he sensed her hesitation, Sean stretched out beside her and braced his weight on one forearm, his upper body above hers. Poised there, he smoothed the hair back from her forehead, the gesture unspeakably tender from such a hard man. "Tell me what you need."

Her inner muscles clenched at the thought of him driving the erection she could feel against her hip deep into her willing body. "More of you."

"How?"

She blinked at the question. "Pardon?"

"Soft and slow? Fast and hard?"

Not soft or gentle. Right now she needed to feel his strength, a little of his roughness. Rather than answer, she smoothed her hands over his back and kissed him hard, letting her hunger speak for itself. Her fingers dug into the muscles in his shoulders, eagerly testing the power thrumming beneath his hot skin. He met the stroke of her tongue eagerly and took over, slowing the kiss to a drugging caress that made her whimper.

All too soon Sean broke the kiss and pressed her down harder into the mattress with his body, holding her there as he studied her face. The tension in his muscles told her just how much he was tempering his response. She could feel the predatory vibe coming from him, the dominant side of him straining for release.

She wriggled beneath him, pressing her hips into the hard ridge of his erection to urge him on. She wanted him to just take control so she could stop thinking. Wanted to feel him filling her, burning away the chill inside her with his heat. A shiver rippled through her at the thought.

But still he didn't peel the shirt over her head like she wanted him to. Instead he sat up on his haunches and watched her, big hands clenching into fists on his thighs.

"Take off your shirt."

Zahra's heart pounded at the soft command. She hadn't expected this authoritative side of him and hesitated an instant before sitting up and reaching for the hem of her thigh-length T-shirt. She started to draw it upward, then stopped. Sean's eyes practically glowed as he stared at her. The air crackled. She wanted to draw this moment out, tease him, make him lose some of that iron control. Her hands inched the soft cotton jersey up her bare thighs, sensitizing every inch of skin with the gentle caress of the fabric. A heavy pulse beat between her legs, her sex growing damp beneath his intense gaze. Then a cool breath of air touched her folds and she stopped again, this time out of uncertainty. Once she crossed this line there was no going back.

"Take it off, Zahra." This time his tone held a warning edge. She'd never seen him like this, so keyed up. A hot thrill shot through her.

The relative dimness helped, but she still fought embarrassment as she edged the hem up farther, exposing the neatly trimmed strip of dark hair between her thighs.

Sean made a low sound and set one hand on her upper thigh, the warmth of his palm and fingers burning her skin, making her core tingle even more. Biting her lip, she studied his face as she drew the shirt upward more, over her stomach and ribs, then over her aching breasts. They felt swollen, heavy, the nipples puckered tight from the cool air and anticipation of his touch. Sean's expression was set, utterly focused on the flesh she'd revealed. She started to pull the shirt over her head, but he stopped her.

"Leave it there."

Swallowing, she lay back against the pillow and watched him study her practically naked body. His heated gaze raked over her flesh before zeroing in on her tight nipples. Nipples that begged for his touch, his mouth. But the strong hand on her thigh never moved.

"How do you like to be touched?"

Zahra swallowed hard. Did he really expect her to answer that? She couldn't spell it out for him, it was too embarrassing. But when she tried to tug his hand away from her thigh, he made a low sound of reassurance and wouldn't budge.

Fighting a wave of self-consciousness, she stared at his bare, chiseled chest. "Softly."

"Mmm," he purred, seeming pleased by her response. "Where?"

The blood rushed to her cheeks. She'd never talked like this to a lover before but she wanted to with Sean. He made her feel sexy and desirable enough to embrace her sexuality. "Here," she whispered, lightly touching a hand to her breast.

His eyes followed the movement with avid interest. "Show me."

A forbidden thrill rushed through her at the erotic challenge in his voice. The command made her feel wickedly hot, and she was more than up for the task. Feeding on the power she gained from teasing him, she raised her hands and let her fingers brush gently back and forth across the lower swells of her breasts. Her skin tingled and warmed beneath her touch, under the potent magic of his gaze.

His eyes stayed locked on her fingers as they whispered over the lush curves of her breasts, driving her arousal higher. When he made no move to touch her, she decided to up the stakes and feathered her fingertips over her hard nipples. A bolt of sensation zinged through her body, ending in the throbbing bud of her clitoris. Zahra arched her back with a little gasp and did it again, pausing this time to grasp the sensitive tips gently between her thumbs and forefingers and squeezing.

"Oh," she whispered, letting her eyes close as her head fell back. She upped the pressure and rolled her nipples, squeezing gently while the pleasure rose steadily inside her, imagining it was his bronzed hands tormenting her so deliciously.

Her eyes snapped open when Sean let out a dark growl. Meeting his hot stare, she licked her lips and kept playing with herself.

"You like to be teased," he said, his tone at once approving and accusing.

Zahra nodded, fighting to keep her breathing calm as she waited to see what he'd do. She wanted his hands on her nipples, wanted him to take them into his mouth. Wanted his fingers sliding into the slick folds between her legs and pushing inside her.

"Does it make you hot to play with yourself while I watch, sweetness?"

"Yes." So hot. More than she'd ever thought possible.

"Show me how much."

Oh God, that deep, velvet voice washing over her. The arousal burning in her overrode any remaining traces of self-consciousness. She started to slide a hand down her belly toward the apex of her thighs, but he stopped her with a shake of his head.

"Spread your legs for me," he murmured. "Show me how wet you are."

Her heart thumped hard against her ribs as the acute sense of vulnerability came rushing back. Opening herself for his perusal made her feel too exposed, too helpless.

His fingers began a slow circle on the top of her thigh, the heat of his touch scalding her skin, sending tingles radiating outward. The pads of his fingers were mere inches from where she was so wet and slippery.

"I...can't." She wanted to submit, but she also needed to resist. Her reaction confused her.

One side of his mouth curved upward, as though he enjoyed her struggle. "No?"

She shook her head, her face so hot it should have glowed in the dimness.

Sean removed his hand from her thigh and reached up to cup her right breast. She closed her eyes in relief and pressed up against his palm, desperate for his touch on her sensitized nipples.

His thumb brushed too softly over the hard nub, making her groan in frustration. "What about now?"

It took a moment for his words to penetrate. "W-what?"

"Do you want to show me now?"

He wasn't going to give this up, she realized. She stared up at him in breathless anticipation, waiting, dying for more of his touch.

His fingers closed around the taut peak and tightened slightly, just enough to make her want to beg. The pressure wasn't enough. She needed more.

"Spread those pretty legs and show me how wet you are, Zahra."

She shook her head again, arching more against his touch. "Please…"

He squeezed more firmly, dragging a throaty moan out of her. Then he rolled it between his fingers, sending off a shockwave of sensation that coalesced into a burning ache in her core. "You want me to make you do it, don't you baby?"

No, she wanted to say. *I don't want that. A good girl wouldn't want that.*

Except she wanted to be bad for him. And he somehow knew it. Somehow understood the dark need rising inside her.

Taking a deep breath, she relented with a nod.

"Good girl," he murmured, rewarding her by reaching up to cup her other breast and give both nipples more stimulation.

"Oh, God."

His low chuckle brushed over her before he released the tender peaks. Zahra jerked her head up to stare at him, but his eyes were intent upon hers as his hands followed the curve of her ribs and stomach to her hipbones. He paused there to caress gently, finding the lines of scar tissue over her surgery sites before skimming down her thighs to her knees. Fighting with herself, dying from the expectation of his touch on the aching bud at the top of her mound, she allowed him to press her knees apart, slowly, her muscles resisting the movement.

When they were far enough apart to let the cool air bathe her heated core, he made a praising sound in his throat. "So gorgeous."

Being on display like this should have shocked her, but instead it only made her wetter. She could feel the moisture gathering, making her slick and ready for him. She closed her eyes, unable to hold his gaze any longer.

"Look at me."

When she didn't obey the quiet command he took her chin in a firm grasp and turned her face toward him. His thumb stroked softly against her lips and she nipped at it, wanting to punish him, make him stop torturing her and just *take* her already. Sean laughed softly.

"Hungry, sweetness? I thought you liked to be teased."

She did, but not this much. Not when she was on fire and craving the thrust of his cock inside her. "Take me."

He shook his head. "I want to see you touch these pretty folds down here," he murmured, his other thumb brushing over the thin strip of hair on her mound. "Put your hand between your legs and show me what feels good."

Her hips lifted in helpless response and her core clenched in near agony. He was pushing her so far she might come from her own fingers, and that's not what she wanted. But damn, she needed to be touched. She hurt with unrelieved need.

Her hands slid over her stomach to her inner thighs and played there gently while he watched with molten eyes. She moved closer to the needy flesh between with ever tightening circles, then her fingers stroked over the open outer lips, up and down until her clit throbbed mercilessly. Panting now, she caressed the inner folds, moving closer to the sensitive bundle of nerves. A moan spilled out when she grazed the edge of it with one fingertip, pleasure swamping her senses.

"That's it, sweetness," Sean whispered, finding her nipples again and tugging on them exactly how she liked.

The pleasure was like a whip on her sensitized body. Zahra whimpered and caressed her clit with two slippery fingers, already feeling a powerful orgasm building. But inside she was aching. Empty.

"That's good, baby. Now slide your fingers inside."

She'd feel depraved later, but right now she couldn't stand the burn any longer. Without hesitation she slid two fingers of her other hand into her body, moaning aloud at the streak of sensation that tore through her. She pumped them in and out slowly, firmly, drawing out the pleasure. It grew and grew, rising up like a tide, the edge of release hovering just over the edge of her consciousness. It wasn't what she wanted but she wasn't going to turn down this chance to pleasure herself in front of him, especially if it turned him on as much as it did her.

"Stop."

On the verge of climax, she froze and opened her eyes to stare at him in disbelief. She was trembling, panting, two fingers buried inside her body, others against her throbbing clit. Reduced to a state of utter wantonness because of how much he'd made her need. "Please," she blurted, not caring that she was begging, mindless with the need for release.

In answer to her plea Sean gently captured her wrists and pulled them from between her thighs, then leaned down to lick her fingers clean. The feel of his tongue, knowing he was tasting her in such an intimate way made her draw in a sharp breath. Her inner muscles clenched at the raw eroticism of the act.

When he looked up at her from between her legs a moment later, she shuddered at the raw lust on his face.

Then he smiled that wickedly sexy smile and whispered, "My turn."

CHAPTER THIRTEEN

Sean knew he was pushing Zahra out of her comfort zone, and it was intentional. Earlier tonight when he'd kissed her he'd seen and felt her startled reaction, as though she'd never experienced this kind of desire before. From her description of her sheltered upbringing and the way she trembled for him now he was convinced this was all new to her, no matter how many men she'd slept with before him. The most primal part of him reveled in that knowledge. He wanted to give her the most intense pleasure of her life, burn himself and this first time for them into her memory forever. Because he wasn't letting her go.

He was also still keyed up from the car chase and knowing he could have lost her. Then Hunter had called a half hour ago to tell him they were following up a possible lead on Amir. Reports indicated it looked like he was on the move, and possibly headed this way. Which had to be a coincidence, because this time only the team members themselves knew where he and Zahra were.

Except Sean didn't believe in coincidence.

He shoved the unsettling thought aside to focus on the here and now. The sweet-tart taste of her was still on his tongue and he wanted more. Zahra was breathing fast, her heavy-lidded gaze locked on his face. Too fucking gorgeous for words.

Leaning forward, he braced his weight on both elbows to cup her luscious breasts in both hands. He bent his head to kiss her silky soft flesh then dragged his tongue up the curves to the stiffened centers. Zahra sank both hands into his hair and arched her back with a quiet gasp as he closed his lips around one nipple and sucked. A ragged groan of relief spilled from her lips as he lavished attention on one, then the other, loving each breathless sound she made and the way her fingers tightened in his hair, holding him close.

When she was squirming and mewling he reluctantly released the captive flesh and kissed his way up the lovely line of her throat and over her jaw to her lips. Zahra turned her head and blindly sought his mouth and he gave it to her, plunging his tongue past her lips as his hands tangled in the spill of her hair. She met each stroke of his tongue, rubbing and rocking against his body in a plea for more. Nipping his way down her jaw and throat, he paused to torment each pouty nipple once more before easing back to admire the view. Stretched out before him, thighs parted to reveal the tender flesh between and her hands gripping his shoulders, she was right out of his fantasies.

Under his stare she started to lower one knee but he blocked it with a hand and opened her again, his eyes fixed on the delectable place between. He could smell how turned on she was and couldn't wait to taste her again. Closing his hands around her ankles he held them firmly and began kissing his way up her calves to her knees, first one leg then the other, playing with his tongue and teeth. At her inner thigh he paused to rub his cheek against her, enjoying the way her muscles tightened beneath his touch.

Keeping hold of her ankles he bent to kiss her taut, quivering abdomen, his tongue stealing out to play with the belly ring she wore. Her muscles twitched beneath his lips and her hands stole into his hair once again. Done with tormenting both of them, Sean placed a gentle kiss on the strip of hair covering her mound. Anticipating the moment she tried to close her legs, he blocked the movement with the width of his shoulders. Zahra bit her lip and watched him wordlessly, that look of anticipation and shyness on her face making him so hard it was painful.

At last he let himself kiss that soft, secret flesh, parting his lips slightly so she could feel the warmth of his breath against her sensitive folds. The muscle tension in her legs told him she was more than ready so he flattened his tongue and licked up the length of her slit in a slow, soft caress. Her lower back arched and her hips came up off the mattress as a ragged cry tore out of her.

Sean closed his eyes to better savor the moment, sliding his tongue into her warmth to get a true taste. Zahra's fingers clenched in his hair and she whimpered, lifting her hips against his mouth.

"So soft, Zahra," he groaned. With a restraining hand splayed out over her belly, he worshipped her with his lips and tongue, focusing on the swollen bud of her clit. He'd watched carefully as she pleasured herself and made sure to mimic the same rhythm and pressure she had. She rewarded his efforts with a ragged moan and opened her thighs farther, allowing him deeper access.

Leaving his hand on her belly, he eased the other one between her legs and worked two fingers into her. Her body squeezed around him, warm and wet. He hooked his fingers upward and stroked with firm pressure along her upper wall.

At her startled cry of pleasure he paused to look up the length of her body. Her eyes were squeezed shut, head turned slightly to one side, her expression one of complete rapture. A moment later her eyes snapped open and focused on him. She opened her mouth to speak but he repeated the movement of his fingers and watched in lust and fascination as she made that same gorgeous face.

Seriously? Had she never found her G-spot before? The idea that he was the first to show her this pleasure pushed him to a new level of possessiveness. Now he grew even more focused, totally determined to blow her mind and enjoy every moment of the show. He stroked her upper wall and licked gently at her clit. Firm fingers, slow, soft tongue.

Her head fell back. "Ohhh, Sean…"

Cock throbbing so badly it was almost unbearable, he stayed with her, allowing her to luxuriate in the sensations as he built her orgasm. He could feel it gathering inside her, see it in the arch of her body, the tension of her belly and thighs, the decadent expression on her face. The sexy mewls and moans she made as she gripped his hair and writhed under his mouth were incredible. A few tender swirls of his tongue, a slight twist of his fingers and…oh yeah.

Her inner muscles rippled then clenched around his fingers. Zahra let loose a loud, sensual cry and started coming, her hands holding him to her in a desperate grip. Sean wasn't going anywhere though. He stayed right with her, softening his mouth only when she melted back against the bed, completely boneless with pleasure.

Breathing hard, he eased back and took a moment to savor the sight of her like that, breasts heaving, face lax with release. Fingers still buried inside her, he shifted to kiss his way back up her body to her breasts and began licking and sucking all over again. Zahra wound her arms around his shoulders and sighed dreamily, stroking his hair. Her sexy little movements told him she was hot and ready for more and he couldn't fucking wait to push into her and make her his completely.

Soft hands roamed over his back and shoulders, up his neck to his head where she scratched sensually against his scalp. "Sean," she whispered, back arching to press her breast harder against his mouth. He obliged her with more pressure against the pouting tip, scraping it with the edge of his teeth. "Sean, take your pants off. I want you inside me."

Oh, fuck, he was gonna come if she kept talking like that.

Pulling back and shifting to his knees, he gently withdrew his fingers and reached for his fly. Zahra lay back against the pillows, watching him as he unzipped and shoved his jeans and boxers down his thighs. She licked her lips when his cock came free, standing straight up against his abdomen. He gripped the base of it tight with one hand and fished in his jeans pocket for the condom he'd stashed there earlier. Twisting to the side to kick his clothes off, he quickly knelt between her thighs and eased her legs around his, placing the soles of her feet on the backs of his calves.

Before he could say anything Zahra reached a slim hand between them and boldly grasped him. The soft, cool touch nearly undid him. Setting his jaw, Sean stared down into her face and closed his hand around hers. He squeezed and stroked her fist over the length of him from base to tip, slowly, then back down. Zahra's gaze was glued to their hands moving over his aroused flesh, the heated fascination in her eyes making the pleasure ten times as intense.

"You're so gorgeous," she whispered.

He might have laughed if he wasn't on the edge of embarrassing himself by coming in her hand. She tested his restraint, that innate sensuality and uninhibited enjoyment destroying his usual control. He'd never wanted anyone the way he wanted—needed—her.

But if he didn't start paying more attention to her pleasure this would be over way too soon and without him getting to feel her coming around his cock. Releasing her hand to give her free reign, he reached up to play with a sensitive nipple while at the same time sliding his free hand between her legs. He rubbed the slick, swollen flesh gently, staying just to the sides of her clit, knowing she'd be sensitive.

Zahra made a crooning sound and kept stroking him, her other hand coming up to pet his chest and belly. Sean groaned softly at the feel of her cool palm against his raging flesh. She glanced up at him and Christ, the look on her face as they pleasured each other sent a warning tingle rocketing up his spine.

Gasping out a breath, Sean pulled her hand away from his cock and grabbed the condom. He tore it open with his teeth and smoothed it on.

"Yes," Zahra whispered, reaching up to grab hold of his shoulders.

Still caressing between her thighs gently, he positioned himself at her opening and looked up at her. Her eyes were locked to where he was rubbing the crown of his cock against her open folds. "You want to watch, sweetness?"

She nodded and licked her lips, never taking her eyes off the erotic sight. Christ that was hot.

Taking himself firmly in hand, Sean pressed slowly and firmly against her. Her body closed around him like a greedy fist, squeezing and rippling around his cock. She whimpered and rocked upward and he drove deep, stretching his body out over hers, weight braced on one forearm beside her head. Her breath caught and Sean stilled, fighting for air while he waited for her body to adjust to him. He knew the moment it did because her hands wound into his hair and she pulled him down for a hungry kiss, their tongues tangling in a slow, sexy exploration. He withdrew a little and began to pump into her, his rhythm steady and forceful as he continued stroking her clit with his fingers.

The low, sexy sounds she made intensified and her thighs contracted around his hips. She lifted into his thrusts, adding an erotic little circle on the downstroke that nearly made his eyes roll back in his head. He allowed himself to plunge deeper, harder, using her moans and sighs as a guide. Soon she was clinging to his shoulders, crying into his mouth, their bodies slick with sweat as they rocked against each other.

Zahra's fingers bit deep into his muscles, the grip of her hands and thighs demanding, desperate. She was close again, so close.

Sean tore his mouth away from hers and buried his face in her throat, struggling to hang on. "Squeeze me," he ordered hoarsely.

Her inner muscles contracted around him and her cries of pleasure filled the room. He rode her hard and deep, fingers moving tenderly around the taut bundle of nerves and she suddenly convulsed around him with a sharp, keening cry. Sean snarled in satisfaction and drove deep, holding himself there as he let go. His orgasm slammed into him, the pleasure all eclipsing, blotting out sight and sound until only sensation remained. His muscles locked, his body shuddering as he came in long, endless waves.

As the ecstasy started to ease he became aware of how stiff Zahra was beneath him and the pained cry she made. Lifting his head he saw the way her face was scrunched up and looked down to see her hand grabbing at her right hip. Sean pushed her hand out of the way and gripped her hip, sinking his fingers deep into the muscle. He eased her thigh out and down with his other hand to alleviate the tension and maintained the pressure there until he felt the spasms ease.

Zahra groaned and went limp beneath him, head turned to one side, eyes closed.

He bent his head to trail kisses along her jaw, up her cheek. "Did I hurt you?"

She shook her head slightly, as though she was too exhausted to move. "Just grabbed right at the end. It's better now, thanks." When she looked at him her hazel eyes were soft with pleasure and lassitude and Sean couldn't help but feel ten feet tall at being the one to put that expression on her face. She lifted a hand to stroke his hair, his cheek. Her tender, languorous smile squeezed his heart. "That was amazing. Unbelievable."

He laughed softly and kissed the heel of her hand. "I'm glad. I thought so too." Sex had never felt like that, ever. He wanted her to crave him, wanted her to become addicted to him so that she'd never be able to walk away once this job was over.

Zahra ran the sole of one foot over the back of his calf in a lazy caress, that beautiful smile still in place. "I've got a lot of lost time to make up for, you know."

He grinned at her. "Yeah?"

She nodded. "I can't wait to see what else I've been missing out on."

Hell, she was tying him in knots and didn't even realize it. He smoothed her hair back from her damp forehead, loving how relaxed she was and how far she'd let herself go with him. "I'll show you anything you want to learn, sweetness."

"Mmm, good." She wound her arms around him and pulled. Sean lowered his weight back onto her, reveling in the feel of her beneath him, her hands running slowly over his naked skin. She kissed his shoulder, the side of his neck, licked at the sensitive spot beneath his ear before gathering him close and hugging tight.

Lying in the cradle of her arms, breathing in her scent and feeling her body wrapped around him, Sean groaned in contentment. "Tired?" she asked, those gentle hands gliding over his back, pausing to squeeze and knead at the sore muscles at the back of his neck. He nearly purred.

"A little. You?" Normally an orgasm made him fall asleep but right now he felt wired, their lovemaking and bond igniting the protective part of him.

"Yeah. I feel like I could sleep for the rest of the day."

"Then you should." Pushing up onto his knees, he gently withdrew from her warmth, smiling at the pout on her face. He pulled the covers up over her and went to the bathroom to ditch the condom. When he came back she was curled onto her side and something about the position made his heart turn over. He was more aware than anyone how strong she was. Seeing her so relaxed and defenseless, knowing she felt safe in his care and trusted him…

God.

Pushing out a breath to ease the pressure in his chest, he lifted the sheets and slid in behind her. Zahra hummed in pleasure and snuggled back into his body, her soft, clean hair tickling his face. Breathing in her scent, one arm wrapped around her waist, Sean let her slide into sleep. Even when her breathing slowed and lengthened and her muscles went lax, he stayed awake to keep careful watch over the woman he was falling in love with.

CHAPTER FOURTEEN

The light was already fading when Amir arrived at the designated spot. Thick clouds obscured the dying sun, a damp breeze washing over the rain soaked streets. With his collar pulled up and his ball cap tugged low on his forehead to ward off the drizzle, he shut his car door and walked slowly toward the warehouse. Probably built in the fifties, it had been deserted long ago along with most of the area. Perfect for what they needed.

He walked up to the side door entrance, his wounded arm aching, the hand and fingers so swollen he could barely move them. A fever had taken hold, leaving him weak and chilled despite the medication he'd taken. As awful as he felt now, it was nothing to what he'd feel if he failed to kill the Titanium team members this time.

After checking to make sure no one was watching, he knocked on the metal door. The pistol in his waistband pressed against his lower back, calming his nerves somewhat. He was fast on the draw; if either of the men he was meeting had murder on their minds, he'd put a bullet straight through their hearts. Amir knew Malik was displeased with him. What he didn't know was whether he'd ordered Amir's death.

The door opened. A light skinned, brown eyed man stood there. He ran a cursory gaze over him. "Amir?"

"Yes. Abdullo?" The Tajik operative Hassani had used as a handler for the previous mission that had resulted in the failed bombing attempt at the Titanium safe house. Apparently Hassani had sent the man here to personally ensure there were no more problems.

The man nodded and stepped back, scanning the area behind Amir. "Come through to the back. We've already loaded everything up."

Amir followed a few steps behind, senses on alert for any threats. In the back of the warehouse an unmarked white van sat in one of the empty bays, lit by an ancient overhead light. A white, twenty-something man with light brown hair stood by the rear doors of the vehicle and slammed them shut as Amir and Abdullo approached.

"This is Bob," Abdullo told him.

"Bob" didn't acknowledge him with anything more than a single glance before walking around to the driver's door. "We going?" Amir was surprised by the total absence of any accent in Bob's speech. Was he American born and raised? He'd expected a Chechen maybe, or someone from the Balkans, however, this man looked like he'd just stepped off the Baltimore docks to be part of this mission. Was he even a Muslim? Amir bristled at the thought of working with an unbeliever, even on this, but he wasn't exactly in a position to protest.

Abdullo gestured impatiently to Amir. "You ride in the back seat."

Pulse elevated, not really sure what to expect, Amir climbed into the back as the other two slid into the front seats. His heart rate slowed slightly when Bob opened the rolling bay door with a remote and drove out into the dull gray evening. They'd been on the road for nearly ten minutes before Amir felt relaxed enough to turn around and get his first look at the weapon strapped in the back.

It was much smaller than he'd expected, about the size of a beer keg. Four of the machines could easily have fit in the back. From the way it was strapped in place it appeared too heavy for a man to carry. Until the call from his handler, after he'd left the prison with a possible location for Zahra, he'd never even known something like this existed, let alone operated one before. Was it even stable? While he wasn't privy to the reasons behind its use on this operation, he figured it had to be some sort of test. Was Hassani planning to use this same kind of device in future attacks or something?

"I'm told you've never worked with anyone else from the group before?" Abdullo asked in English, he assumed for Bob's benefit.

Amir found a certain ironic amusement in Abdullo's polite term for the cell. It made them sound so civilized, as though they weren't part of a militant terrorist organization. "No."

"Well, no matter. Once we deliver the device you'll stay with it. When we're out of range we'll text you. You'll activate it and then go hunting on foot. We'll come back to pick up the device."

"And leave me there?" he asked sardonically, already seeing how this was going to play out.

"If you can kill the targets and make it back to the drop off point in time to meet us, you're welcome to ride back with us. If not, you'll have to find your own way back."

Amir didn't plan on meeting up with them. He was certain they'd just kill him after he'd activated the device, and dump his body in the woods somewhere. No, he'd make his own way out of the forest and stay far away from Baltimore.

If he wanted to live, that meant avoiding both American authorities and Hassani's network. He had to go off the grid and stay off.

He was curious about Bob but didn't bother asking how he fit into all this. Was he just an average American who'd been lured by the promise of a big pay day for this op? Or did he have some sort of military training? The weapon was top secret classified, and must have been either stolen from a military installation or purchased on the black market. Amir had no idea how Hassani had managed to obtain one, let alone a portable one, though his connections were legendary.

That's why Amir had good reason to keep his guard up.

Though the meeting point had been set far outside of the city, the tension-filled two hour drive passed far too slowly for his liking. When Amir saw the sign welcoming them to Deep Creek Lake, his palms grew damp. The heavy rains all day had made the ground soft but fortunately this road was well traveled enough that no one would find the tire marks in the mud unusual.

Hiding the device was another matter.

Bob drove them around the lake to a secluded part of the forest just under a mile from the target house. They took an access road all the way to the end, and finding no buildings or signs of habitation, drove back partway. The van stopped on the leaf-carpeted shoulder and Bob switched off the lights and ignition.

"Everyone out," Abdullo ordered.

Amir eased out of the van, careful to hide his grimaces of pain each time his wound was jarred. The rain had stopped but moisture dripped from the leaves with gentle patters. He walked around to the back and watched as the other men unloaded the weapon from the cargo area. Both men wore thick gloves. They grunted and strained to lift the thing between them. Once they unloaded it they hauled it into the woods, their passage made difficult by rocks and fallen trees.

Amir followed them farther and farther into the shadows until they eventually stopped and carefully set the device down on a thick carpet of decaying leaves. His good hand itched to curl around the grip of his pistol but he wasn't worried about them killing him yet. Not before he could activate the secret weapon and carry out the hits he was responsible for.

Sweating and panting, Abdullo ran a sleeve across his forehead. "Come here."

Amir approached, stopping a foot from the hunk of metal. It looked like something out of a science fiction movie and part of him didn't believe it was capable of doing what he'd been told it did.

"This is the button to arm it. This one is to activate it. Once you receive our text, you must reply to us before you arm it, so we know when the attack is about to take place. It's already been programmed with the correct code."

Amir nodded. "How long until you'll be out of range?"

"Twenty minutes or so."

That long? This thing must have a wider range than he'd imagined. It would give him more lead time to escape though.

"Good luck." Abdullo started back for the van, Bob right behind him.

Soon they were swallowed up by the forest. Amir waited, straining to hear anything other than the fading birdsong and the drip of water then finally he caught the muted sound of an engine starting. He pulled out his phone to mark the time, already anticipating a text in twenty minutes that would signal the start to the operation. As handy and as much a modern miracle as it was, his Smartphone would be useless soon. The moment he activated the weapon he and everyone else within range would be plunged back into the Stone Age.

Zahra stepped out of the bathroom dressed in a pair of jeans and a blue sweater Claire had loaned her. The jeans were baggy on her and too long in the leg, the sweater hanging on her frame, but she was just grateful to have something to wear. Not that being naked around Sean was a hardship. After the way he'd made love to her, she was looking forward to getting naked with him again the first chance she got.

Smiling at the thought, she emerged into the kitchen to find him working on a laptop at the small round table nestled into the nook by the front windows. Her hip was still tender and her neck and shoulders were stiff but she had the most delicious soreness between her legs that served as a constant reminder of how Sean had possessed her. That hadn't been sex. She'd had enough of that to know the difference, and what she and Sean had shared had been so emotional and beautiful it made her tingle all over to remember it.

He glanced up when he heard her and the smile he flashed her nearly took her breath away. "How do you feel? Sleep okay?"

"Slept great." Almost all day, as it turned out. It was already past dinner time. "And I feel amazing, considering we were in a pretty bad car wreck last night." She walked up and bent to slide her arms around his chest from behind, pressing her cheek into the side of his neck. "But I'm pretty sure I feel amazing because of what you did to me."

"Sweetness, you were amazing long before I did that, trust me."

Zahra kissed the side of his neck and slid her hands over the contours of his chest, down to his flat, hard stomach. Sean made a quiet sound of enjoyment and tipped his head to the side so she could nibble and caress, his big hands covering hers as he urged her to explore all those sexy muscles hidden beneath his T-shirt.

Lord, he smelled good, like soap and musk. She could eat him up. Continuing to pet him, she peered over his shoulder at the laptop. "Working on anything interesting?"

"I don't remember," he answered, eyes closed as her hands roamed over him. "Can't remember anything with you touching me."

She laughed softly but it was a secret thrill to know she affected him as much as he did her. This new sense of feminine power was heady and she could see herself getting addicted to making him purr and arch into her touch. As her hands slid low on his abdomen she felt the muscles clench and an answering throb began between her legs. She let her palms stroke over his denim clad thighs, savoring the power in the bunching muscles beneath her skin. The hard ridge of his erection was outlined against the fly of his jeans and she imagined walking around to kneel between his spread thighs, unzipping him and pulling him out. She'd wrap her fingers around him and stroke him the way he'd taught her, then bend her head and take that gorgeous plump head into her mouth. He'd tangle his hands in her hair and let his head fall back, praise her with whispered words and guttural male groans of pleasure as she sucked him like a lollipop.

Gentle hands closed around her wrists, stopping her exploration. "And I'm gonna forget my own damn name if you don't stop that."

Blushing but intrigued, she allowed him to pull her hands away and tug her to stand next to him. His dark eyes glowed with banked desire as he looked up at her. "Behave and stop distracting me while I get some work done, and I'll reward you for your patience later."

The sensual heat in the words sent a shiver through her. She couldn't wait to see what he had in mind for "later".

When he kissed the inside of both wrists and released them, she drew a shaky breath and ran a hand through her damp hair. "You hungry?"

The look he slanted her almost melted her knees.

"For food," she clarified with a laugh. "I thought I'd make some pancakes with fruit or something."

He raised one black eyebrow. "I thought you had a thing against serving guys food?"

She flushed, remembering her snappish comment to him last week. It seemed so bitchy now. "I do. But for you I might make an exception from time to time."

He smiled again, this time in that lopsided grin that made her heart squeeze. "In that case, I'd love some pancakes, thanks."

"Then keep working and I'll see what I can do." She rummaged through the fridge to pull out what she needed. Mixing the batter, she looked back at the laptop. "More encryption?"

"Yeah. Hunter and the others are out doing recon on 'Amir'. They think he's moving west but they don't know to where or why, and he didn't report in to work at the cab company this morning. It's possible he was in that pickup last night."

Zahra went cold inside. Putting a name to the shooter last night made it that much more vivid somehow. "Did you hit him, do you think? Maybe he didn't go into work because he's wounded?"

"Dunno, but the guys are checking into all that. Alex thinks if I can hack into this forum, we might find some more answers about who Amir really is and who he's working for. The security on this one's a bitch, though."

He didn't seem overly concerned about the whole Amir thing, so she relaxed and let it go. "Well, shout if you need a hand with that."

One side of his mouth curved upward, his attention back on the screen as he typed away. "Will do."

Zahra melted butter in a pan and waited for it to sizzle before adding the first ladle of batter. While she waited for bubbles to appear around the edges she began cutting up some strawberries and bananas Sean had bought them. She'd just flipped the pancake over when Sean's phone rang. He pushed back from the table to grab it from his pocket and answered.

"What?" he said sharply a moment later.

Zahra turned to look at him, fingers frozen around the spatula. He pushed his chair back with a loud scrape and stood up, the line of his shoulders pulled taut beneath his shirt. Her pulse accelerated.

"When?" A demand, not a question. His face was grim, anger radiating from every line of his body.

Zahra instinctively reached out and shut off the burner, shoving the pan aside. Something told her they wouldn't be eating anytime soon.

"Yeah, got it. I'll let you know."

He disconnected and faced her. "That was Alex. The FBI just contacted him to say they found a solid lead on Amir."

She stared at him, filled with a growing sense of foreboding, distantly aware of her heart pounding in her ears.

"Apparently he paid your father a visit at the prison this morning."

CHAPTER FIFTEEN

Sean didn't know what the fuck was going on but he didn't intend to wait here and see what happened. "Does your father still know about this place?" he demanded. "That you still own it?"

Zahra's face blanched, her pupils dilating. One hand flew to her throat. "I…maybe. I don't know."

That was all he needed to hear. "Get your stuff. We're leaving."

She hesitated only a fraction of a second before hurrying toward her bedroom. Sean muttered a curse and ran his hand through his hair. According to Alex, by the time the FBI was alerted about the prison visit and someone had translated the recorded conversation between Ibrahim Gill and Amir, this new threat to Zahra had materialized a few hours ago. They'd talked about a woman, and Amir was desperate to find her.

Even with the last part of the recording unintelligible, Sean and Alex were both concerned that Ibrahim might have given Amir the cabin's location. Sean was going to move Zahra immediately and head out of state to another safe house. This time they were going dark, as soon as he informed Alex of their final location.

He powered down the laptop and snapped it shut, hurriedly shoving it into its backpack case. He found Zahra in her room straightening the bed and her bag all packed and zipped at the foot of it. "Ready?" he asked.

"Just need to grab a few things from the bathroom." She hurried away.

Already wearing what he'd brought with him, Sean grabbed the bag and his duffle and started for the front door, pulling out his phone to call Hunter. He explained what had happened and what the plan was. "I'll text or call you once I know where we're going."

"We'll come to you. We're only a half hour away from you anyway, following a trail Amir left us."

He let out a relieved breath, glad to know they'd have back up nearby if they needed it. "All right. We'll contact you once we're back on the highway and we can set up a rendezvous point."

"Roger that. You got enough firepower with you for the moment?"

"Yeah, for the time being—" Just as he gripped the door knob, all the lights went out. He stilled. His phone wasn't working either. What the hell?

"Sean?" Zahra called out from the bathroom.

"I'm still here," he answered. A glance out the front windows showed the opposite side of the lake was also pitch black. Unease slid through him. "Zahra, check your phone."

A pause. "It's not working. I just charged the battery."

Just to be sure he wasn't being completely paranoid, he dug out his laptop and tried to power it up. Nothing.

"Looks like the whole lake's out," Zahra commented from the hallway.

Sean straightened. There was only one thing he knew of that would cut power and disable electronic devices. An electromagnetic pulse could be natural, could be from a powerful explosion…and it could also be used as a weapon.

His heart rate accelerated. "Leave all your stuff. We have to go, now."

"Why, what's happening?" she asked as she came out of the bathroom.

"I think we just got hit with an EMP burst."

"Are you serious?" she asked incredulously.

"Yeah." And if it had been some kind of attack, it was too much of a coincidence to believe it wasn't to target them. A non-nuclear EMP strike had a limited range, so if it was manmade, the culprits had to be close. Which meant he was getting Zahra the hell away from this cabin. "Come here, quick."

She came over and set a hand on his shoulder to orient herself. Sean opened his duffle and started unloading his weapons and ammo. He had a tactical flashlight in there as well, but using it now would light them up like a spotlight.

"Sean…"

He heard the fear in her voice and reached up to squeeze her hand once in reassurance. "Take this," he said, placing a SIG in her palm. She sucked in a breath but before she could argue he continued. "If someone's waiting out there I need you to be able to defend yourself if necessary."

He quickly explained how to remove the safety and that a shot was already loaded into the chamber. He ran through how to fire it, placing her hands on the weapon to point everything out as he did so. "If you need to shoot, wrap both hands around the grip and overlap them, like this." Her fingers were cold beneath his. "Keep it tucked into the back of your pants. When we leave here you need to stay right behind me, I mean right on my ass. Understand?"

"Yes," she whispered.

He pulled out the M4 and slung it around his shoulders, grabbed several magazines and stuffed them into his pockets. The electronic gear and NVGs he'd packed were totally useless now. Their vehicle was useless. He'd spotted a boat with an old outboard motor tied to a dock about a quarter mile away but using it to get across the lake wouldn't help them since the power was out there as well.

They were on their own now, cut off from everyone who could help them, and moving blind against an unseen enemy. Even if Hunter figured out something was wrong and came racing to the rescue, Sean wasn't sure how he'd find his team members without having some form of communication device. "You ready?"

"Yeah."

"Once we walk through that door talk in as soft a whisper as you can, and only when you absolutely need to."

"Okay."

"Get on your stomach and stay down for a minute." He heard her shifting into position and opened the door. Stepping cautiously out onto the front porch he pressed his back against the wooden exterior. Absolute silence greeted him, only the rustle of the wind in the trees breaking it. A damp breeze ruffled the surface of the lake and brushed across his face. Visibility was the shits, but it wasn't zero. The darkness could be used to their advantage. Having Zahra with him was gonna be a challenge though. He could move like a ghost through this kind of terrain; she couldn't, and her limp would make her progress even noisier to anyone with training.

He eased around the side of the cabin, using all his senses to scan the immediate area. When no shots or noises alerted him, he went back to the door and pushed it open. "Okay, we're clear. Let's go." He took her hand and pulled her to her feet. She followed, probably scared but staying put would leave them easy targets. Moving was the only way to protect her now. They'd have to hike out of the area on foot and call for backup once they reached the edge of the damage zone—however big that was.

The wooden steps creaked slightly beneath his weight. He paused to lean down and put his mouth against Zahra's ear. "Don't drag your feet when you move. Try to make as little noise as possible." When she nodded he straightened and took her hand, the other wrapped around the M4.

Skirting the edge of the property, he aimed for a diagonal route to the road through the trees for added cover. Once they were concealed he paused again to assess the road. Nothing moved or carried on the breeze, and any vehicle within range would be out of commission. He tugged on Zahra's hand. She stayed right behind him as they rushed across the road and into the woods on the other side. He chose a southeast route, the shortest and most direct line to the nearest highway. Placing each step carefully on the forest floor, he led her behind him, wincing every time she snapped a twig or disturbed something on the ground, the noises sounding amplified to his ears.

A hunter would easily pinpoint their location. And the itch between his shoulder blades told him they were being hunted.

Zahra stumbled over something. Sean whipped around to catch her and keep her from falling. No sooner had he closed his arms around her than the sharp crack of a pistol shattered the quiet. Instantly he shoved Zahra flat on the ground and covered her with his body. She was completely still beneath him, hardly even breathing, every muscle rigid.

Sean lifted his head slightly and strained to hear in the darkness. That shot had come from their rear and slightly to the left. Other than the darkness, their only cover was some thin tree trunks, and he wasn't willing to drag Zahra up to run and make a bigger target for whoever was out there. Shifting slowly, he eased onto his side long enough to bring his rifle up into position and lay flat beside Zahra.

A faint rustle came from the brush up ahead. Sean honed in on it and raised the muzzle, finger resting on the trigger. A full minute passed before he heard it again; a slight disturbance in the underbrush, this time to his ten o'clock. The instinct to move Zahra was strong, but the training ingrained in him took over. He stayed in place, stock still, waiting for the enemy to make a mistake and expose himself.

The sound came again, closer, now at his eleven o'clock. Was the bastard trying to sneak around them on the left? Sean held the advantage now. He was in his element, able to stay still and silent for hours on end. Whoever was hunting them clearly didn't have either the discipline or patience to do the same. And that would be their undoing.

Whoever it was came nearer yet, less than seventy-five yards away as best Sean could tell. They were still circling to the left, almost at nine o'clock. Leaning over, Sean set his mouth against Zahra's ear. "Stay here. Don't move 'til I come for you," he breathed, careful not to let his words carry. No telling how many others were out scouring the woods for them. At her nod he inched his way forward on his belly. On a stalk he could sneak up on a trained instructor looking for him with a pair of high-powered binoculars. This careless piece of shit hunting them didn't stand a chance against him.

Moving slow and stealthily he eased his way around Zahra and took up position between her and the shooter. Normally when he was in combat nothing broke his concentration but part of his attention remained on Zahra, who thankfully hadn't moved from where he'd left her. Out in front of him the shooter was still concealed and didn't seem to be moving anymore. Using a thin log as a shooting platform, Sean braced the butt of the M4 against his shoulder and waited.

Moments later, movement in the trees to his left alerted him. Adjusting his aim, he curled his index finger around the trigger. In the thin moonlight a branch moved in the distance, maybe fifty yards away. Sean zeroed in on the spot as best he could and slowed his breathing, getting ready to fire between heart beats. Another rustling sound, followed by the shifting of another branch. Something scurried across the ground behind him, near Zahra. He whipped his head around in time to see a raccoon run past her.

Three shots rang out in rapid succession, close enough that he heard them whizz by before plowing into the earth to his right, way too fucking close to Zahra.

Sean caught the muzzle flash of the last shot, adjusted his aim and squeezed the trigger. Two rounds punched from the muzzle of the rifle with sharp cracks. An instant later the sound of a body crashing to the ground followed. No moans or cries of pain came. Whether he'd hit the guy or just scared him, he couldn't tell. Was he dead? Sean held his position, ready to fire again the moment he had a target.

He got his answer soon enough when he heard more twigs snapping as the shooter hauled ass away from him. Though he could have tried hitting him again, with hardly any ambient light and Zahra to think of, their best option was to get as far away from the asshole as possible. Alone he could have done things much differently, but not with her here.

In a low crouch Sean rushed back to Zahra and grabbed her by the arm to haul her to her feet. "Move," he commanded in a whisper, spine tingling in a silent warning that they were still in danger.

"Did you hit him?" she whispered back, hurrying after him.

"Don't know." He hoped so, because he liked the thought of the shooter bleeding and suffering for his part in coming after Zahra. "Just run."

She did, jogging in his wake while tightly gripping his hand. Branches slapped at them as they raced through the forest. Sean didn't know how far they had to go before they hit a decent sized road where they might be able to flag down help. Until then he'd just have to hope they could avoid detection by anyone else hunting them.

Amir crashed through the underbrush, intent on getting around and ahead of his prey. It was so dark he could barely see. Those bullets had missed him, but not by much and it terrified him how close he'd just come to dying without realizing it. Not only was Zahra's bodyguard armed, he was a lethal shot even in near total darkness. The likelihood of killing both targets seemed improbable. But he had to try.

He ran along the inside of the tree line, intending to take a shortcut down a path he'd traveled earlier, when he heard the sound of a vehicle moving down the road. Surprised that anything was working in the area, he realized it must have come from outside the weapon's radius. A plan formed in his mind. He'd carjack it and head for the next road over. Sooner or later his prey would have to cross it if they were to get to the main highway.

He changed direction and headed for the vehicle but stopped as it turned up an access road and disappeared in the screen of trees. From the track of its headlights he could see where it was and it was driving toward the weapon. Amir ran toward it at an angle so he could jump out in front of it, his pistol held steady in his good hand. Just as he was closing in on it the vehicle—a dark minivan—picked up speed. Cursing, he changed direction again and charged after it. Up ahead somewhere he lost sight of it and soon the engine stopped. He rushed on anyway, needing the mobility that vehicle would provide him. A possible getaway car if all else failed.

He was in mid-stride, jumping over a fallen log when he heard the sound of the van's hatch shutting. Skidding to a stop, he dropped to his knees and stared in suspicion at the scene before him.

Someone had retrieved the weapon.

Unless someone else had managed to find out where it was, which he doubted, as far as he was aware only three people knew its location. Fear twined its icy fingers around the base of his spine. There was only one reason a team would be sent in to recover it now. A cleanup operation, meant to sterilize the area and remove all evidence of the plot.

Amir's heart seized for a moment as he realized that Zahra Gill and her bodyguard were no longer the only prey in this dark forest tonight.

CHAPTER SIXTEEN

Zahra smothered a gasp when Sean stopped abruptly and crouched down. She sank down beside him, finally understanding what had alerted him. A vehicle driving nearby. The screen of trees was too thick for her to see it but it sounded fairly close. Pulling in slow, silent breaths despite the pounding of her heart, she waited beside Sean, wondering if this was a new threat. Were others coming after them now?

Moments later she heard the sound of a door or hatch shutting, then silence. No one started the engine again, which didn't bode well because they were in the middle of nowhere.

At a sharp tug on her hand she followed Sean away from where the vehicle was. The sounds seemed augmented when everything else was so hushed and still. She was amazed at how quiet he was, while she felt like a hippo bulldozing its way through the woods.

Moving so stealthily was agonizingly slow, especially with potential shooters so close. Placing each foot carefully where Sean stepped she stayed close behind him and tried to keep her breathing quiet. The terrain dipped into a wide hollow. Three steps down, her foot caught on something and she slid. Catching herself on Sean's shoulder, she winced at the noise she'd just made. He was preternaturally still, no doubt trying to determine if her bumbling had just exposed them. Her heart shot into her throat when she heard loud whispers behind them in the darkness. Two people, the low timbre suggesting they were men. Her heart knocked against her ribs. Would someone coming after them risk blowing their cover that way? Either they weren't a threat at all, or they were so confident in their ability that giving themselves away didn't matter.

Sean pulled on her hand and she obediently went to one knee beside him. When he put a solid hand against her back she understood what he wanted and laid flat on her belly. He pressed his palm between her shoulder blades once, hard, in a silent command to stay put. In the natural depression she had better concealment than she had before. It still went against every instinct to lie there while Sean moved away from her.

Reminding herself that whoever was in the screen of trees wasn't necessarily a threat, she tried to relax and slow her heart rate. In the near darkness she barely caught sight of Sean as he crawled out of the gully and disappeared over the far edge. The moment he did, fear began to take hold. She reached one hand back and withdrew the gun from her waistband, holding it the way Sean had shown her in that lightning fast tutorial before they'd left the cabin.

The blood rushed loudly in her ears and her palms turned cold and damp. She had no idea where Sean was now, or when he'd be coming back. A slight disturbance in the undergrowth caught her attention. She turned her head to the side, holding her breath as she tried to ascertain the source. Was it one of the men? It took all her self control to remain there, flattened against the damp ground. Her jeans and sweater were soaked through. She shivered in the cool damp air.

There it came again, off to her right. She tracked it, every second feeling like an eternity. Then something else moved just out of sight, but almost directly in front of her this time.

Two of them. Circling around. Her fingers tightened around the cool grip of the pistol. She fumbled to get her finger gingerly in place around the trigger, her heart somersaulting in terror. Thankfully whoever it was kept moving, she hoped because they didn't realize she was even there. But where the hell was Sean?

Both men continued past her position, seeming to move deeper into the trees. Her muscles, already sore and tight from the accident, began to knot from the strain of holding still for so long. She bit down on the inside of her cheek and squeezed her eyes shut to hold back a groan when her right hip grabbed suddenly. Sweating and panting in the grip of the excruciating spasm, Zahra struggled to stay silent. She rolled a little to one side in the hopes of easing it and jerked when a branch snapped to her left. Focusing on that sound, she breathed through her mouth and didn't dare move.

She jumped when shots cracked through the night out in front of her. Farther away than she would have expected. Three more quick shots followed from the right, then the deeper bark of a rifle answered with two closely-spaced shots. A muffled grunt of pain followed. Had Sean hit one of them? Was he okay?

No sooner had the thought formed than more shooting erupted. Two separate weapons, the shooters moving constantly. Her heart thudded painfully in her chest. She tried to comfort herself with the knowledge that it was so dark they likely couldn't see Sean any better than he could see them. All the while she was aware of the other person creeping up to her left.

Sean fired again, the muzzle flash hidden from view. The other shooters returned fire, shooting sporadically. Had they seen Sean's position when he'd fired?

Another branch snapped beside her. She almost stopped breathing when a figure emerged out of the trees at the edge of the hollow, less than twenty feet to her left. Terror flooded her system, flashing hot then freezing cold over her skin. Her instincts screamed at her to run, but she knew that would be suicide.

The man moved slowly and when the clouds broke for a moment she caught sight of his silhouette outlined against the sky. He was holding a pistol in one hand, his face looking straight ahead. She held her breath as he paused. But when shots sounded up ahead once more, he crouched low and kept moving as though he meant to pass her.

He hadn't seen her.

Relief crashed over her in a dizzying wave, but it quickly faded as he continued toward where Sean had gone. She cast a desperate glance ahead of her, her line of sight completely obscured by the edge of the small gully. Everything in her told her to scream a warning. She refused to cave in to that need, knowing she'd be shot dead before Sean could even move.

The gun felt cold and foreign in her grip. But there was no other option for her now. She had to shoot this enemy down before he could pose another threat to Sean. More shots rang out in the trees ahead and Sean's rifle answered from a different position than last time.

Shaking, she raised the pistol and curled her finger around the trigger, applying pressure. She must have made a sound because the man whirled, his gun trained in her direction and Zahra's mouth went dry. Aiming it at his torso she pulled the trigger, the gun kicking in her hand as he fired back. She cried out at a burning sensation in her left calf and rolled to the side in reflex just as his strangled shout of pain registered. He dropped heavily to his knees and Zahra took her chances.

She got up and ran for her life.

The burn in her leg barely registered as she careened up the far bank of the gully. With every step she expected a bullet to plow into her spine, but there was no way she was stopping. "Sean!" she yelled.

Seconds later a pair of steely arms grabbed her around the ribs and a hard body tackled her to the ground. Opening her mouth to scream, a rough palm clamped over her lips.

"Zahra, *shh*."

She froze at the sound of Sean's voice, not even caring that from his tone he was beyond livid with her. She shoved at his hand, aware for the first time that no one was shooting at them.

"Another shooter," she blurted out in a whisper. "I hit him but he's right behind me."

He tensed and jerked his head up to scan behind her but nothing disturbed the silence. "Just run," he ordered, dragging her up.

"What about the others?" she whispered back, running as fast as her abused legs would carry her.

"Down," he snapped, and kept running.

The adrenaline flooding her body lasted for another few minutes before it began to wane. Pain shot up her calf with every step, the muscles in her right hip screaming at her to stop. *No way in hell.*

Soon her strides faltered, her wounded leg too weak and painful to carry her. She gasped and shot a hand out for Sean before she fell.

He slowed and steadied her. "Are you hurt?"

"A little," she managed through gritted teeth, determined to keep going. The road was up ahead somewhere, they had to be close.

Before she realized what he was doing Sean pivoted and set a solid shoulder into her stomach, lifting her right off her feet. She gripped the back of his shirt to balance herself and hung on, biting down on her lower lip to keep from crying out every time his running gait jarred her wound. Silently she urged him to run faster, to escape the shooter still waiting behind them in the trees.

As the running footsteps traveled away from him, Amir staggered upright and braced his weight against a tree. His belly burned, blood streaming from the bullet wound, leaving him nauseated and dizzy. She'd shot him. That bitch had damn well gut shot him. He couldn't tell how far in the bullet had gone but it hurt like hell and he was bleeding like crazy. How had he not seen her lying there? He'd been so intent on escaping Abdullo and "Bob" that he'd run straight past her without realizing it.

Gasping for air, he forced his rubbery legs to carry him through the trees toward the road. He'd been lucky her bodyguard had been too busy picking off the others to get a clean shot at him. Either Amir kept moving or he'd eat a final bullet from him.

Behind him he could hear the sound of footsteps following him. Whether it was Zahra or her bodyguard or one of the others, it didn't matter. His only chance now was to get to the road and hope someone found him before his enemies did.

He barely felt his feet moving, too consumed with fear and the hellish burning in his gut. If he didn't stop the bleeding somehow he'd probably die before he reached the damn road. Hard pressure against the spot made sparks dance before his eyes. He *had* to keep moving, no matter how much it hurt. Blindly he pushed himself, losing track of everything but the pain and the direction he needed to go in.

He struggled onward for what seemed like forever before the trees began to thin. His feet touched grass. Blinking, he realized he'd finally made it to the road. With a strangled groan he sank to his knees and prayed for a passerby to come along.

He didn't know how much time passed. At first he thought he was hallucinating when he spotted the headlights approaching. Bracing himself against the pain, he struggled to his feet and lurched a step out onto the asphalt. The vehicle's headlights hit him, lighting him up from head to toe. He didn't have the strength to hold up an arm to flag them down, and remained standing in the middle of the road. Ahead, the vehicle began to slow.

Relief trickled through him, overwhelming the fear and pain. He didn't even care about going to prison anymore as long as he got medical treatment. The vehicle was close enough now for him to see it was a dark SUV. Totally different from what the other cell members had picked up the weapon with. His muscles began to sag.

The SUV roared up and screeched to a stop in front of him. But Amir's relief was short lived when the doors popped open. Instead of a good Samaritan, three big men holding weapons exploded from it and bore down on him.

"Freeze!" one of them barked.

He weakly raised one hand to show he was unarmed but couldn't speak. As the men closed in on him he saw their faces in the beam of the headlights and his brain suddenly cleared. The other three members of the Titanium team. A hysterical, ironic laugh bubbled up. Rescuers or executioners? While the two white men held him at gunpoint, the one with darker skin stalked over and roughly slammed him face first onto the road. He hit with a grunt that turned into a guttural shriek of pain as the bullet wounds seared him. The sniper—Ellis, he remembered blearily—shoved his arms behind his back and dug his knee into Amir's spine.

He patted him down and then hauled him upright once again. Amir swayed in the man's grip. He heard Ellis speaking to the other two, felt himself being dragged toward the vehicle and couldn't summon the energy to fight. Ripping sounds followed and someone pressed a dressing to his belly.

Distantly he caught the sound of another vehicle. More doors slammed. Voices swirled above him, around him. Then someone snatched him by the front of his shirt and snarled in his face. "Where's Zahra?"

His eyes snapped open. A man with graying hair and deadly silver eyes stared back at him, his face pinched with fury.

"Where is she?" he yelled, giving him a threatening shake.

"Ran...away," he managed, too far gone to keep his mouth shut. All he wanted was for the pain to stop.

"Where?" the man snarled.

"W-woods." The fist knotted in his shirt gripped harder, then shoved him again and let go.

"Find them," Amir heard him growl to the others.

His eyes slid closed once more as the man giving him medical attention pulled a tourniquet around his arm and poked a needle into his forearm. Everything began to fade away, the grip of the pain easing, and he welcomed it. Maybe death was preferable after all to what he'd face if he survived this.

CHAPTER SEVENTEEN

Nearing the edge of the tree line, Sean stopped to make sure they weren't being followed. He shifted Zahra on his shoulder, aware of the blood streaming from her left lower leg. The lower part of his shirt and his jeans were wet with it and he could smell the iron tang on the air.

Once he was certain no one was coming after them, he eased her to the ground and reached between his shoulder blades to peel his shirt off, then knelt before her. "Let me see," he whispered, grasping her left ankle. She flinched but didn't fight him as he rolled her pant leg up and out of the way.

Blood glistened darkly in the faint moonlight filtering through the trees. Zahra hissed in a breath and grasped his hand when he tested the wound. The bullet had torn a chunk away from the back of her calf, about halfway up. Since she'd been running on it he was pretty sure it wasn't broken but flesh wounds hurt like hell. "Hold still." He wrapped the shirt around the wound and tied it as tightly as he could to staunch the bleeding, hardening his heart against her pain.

From his back pocket he pulled out the flip-style cell phone he'd taken off one of the dead shooters, and dialed

Hunter's number. "Where are you?" Sean asked when Hunter picked up.

"We're here, and we've got Amir. Where are you?"

Sean gave him his best guess based on what he knew of the area.

"We're less than a mile from you. Either of you hurt?"

"Zahra was hit in the leg." His throat was tight as he said it. He fucking hated that he hadn't been there to take out the third shooter, hated even more that she'd been hurt on his watch, and by a gun. "I think it's only a flesh wound though."

"Your six clear?"

"Not sure. There were three of them in there. I took one out and hit the other. If you've got Amir then there might be one more out there somewhere."

"Zahra shot Amir."

"She did?"

"Yeah. Right in the gut."

A fierce satisfaction rose inside him. She amazed him. He set a hand on her shoulder, rubbed to help stem the tremors that raced over her skin. "He going to make it?" They needed to question him.

"Doubt it. We're rolling to you now. You should see us in the next minute or so."

"Roger that." And fuck, he'd be glad to see them. "One more thing."

"Go ahead."

"They used an EMP weapon of some kind. That's why my phone died in the middle of our convo."

"You're shitting me."

"Nope. Has to be nearby. Get what you can out of Amir before he croaks."

"With pleasure."

Disconnecting, Sean snapped the phone shut and reached out to gather Zahra into his lap. "You got him, sweetness. Got him good."

She nodded against his shoulder, her body vibrating from a combination of shock and cold. Sean was so fucking proud of her for overcoming her fear and aversion to firearms and protecting herself like that. It couldn't have been easy for her.

He buried his face in the cool silk of her hair. "I'm sorry I wasn't there."

"It's ok-kay."

No it wasn't. She'd been forced to shoot to save herself and been wounded in turn because he'd left her alone. If the shooter had had more light, she would've died. The guilt sat on his chest like an anvil. Keeping his ears cocked for any danger, he cradled her against his chest and willed Hunter and the others to hurry the fuck up.

Finally the distant rumble of an engine met his ears. Sure enough, moments later headlights appeared over the crest of a hill. Recognizing the outline of the government issued SUV, he relaxed. He scooped Zahra up and pushed to his feet, carrying her out of the trees to the edge of the road. The vehicle raced up and stopped next to them. Gage popped out from behind the wheel and Hunter from the passenger side, Ellis and Alex from the back.

Hunter and Ellis were suited up with body armor and NVGs, rifles at the ready. "Okay?" Hunter asked as he approached.

"Yeah, but she'll be better once we get the bleeding stopped," Sean answered, carrying her toward the back. Alex stood at the rear, lowering the tailgate for him. In the overhead light Sean could see the worry etched into the lines of the man's face as he scanned Zahra.

Sean gently set her inside the back as Alex leaned in. "Ambulance is on its way, but it's at least forty minutes out," he said, reaching out to grab one of Zahra's hands.

"No, no ambulance," she protested, wincing as she scooted back. "Please, my leg's not broken and Sean says it's only a flesh wound."

"I didn't mean *only* as in it's no big deal. You still need to be patched up," Sean told her, unwrapping his sodden shirt from her calf.

She stifled a moan when he pulled it away from the wound and Sean got his first look at the damage. It'd been a while since he'd had to use the medical training he'd received in the military. The bullet had entered the outside of her left calf and torn its way across the fleshy part beneath the gastrocnemius muscles. It was ugly but not serious, though she'd have a hell of a scar back there once it all healed. The wound bled steadily without pumping out, so he was pretty sure no arteries had been damaged.

"How bad is it?" she asked, wiping the back of her hand over her damp upper lip.

"You're gonna need a few stitches."

"Can't we just drive to the hospital? I don't want to wait out here anymore. Or can't one of you just stitch me now and then take me to the hospital?"

Yeah, they could, and Sean didn't blame her for wanting the hell away from here. Truth be told, he didn't like leaving them exposed on this road for a second longer than necessary. Other attackers might be nearby or en route. He pinched the edges of the wound together, ignoring the pained growl Zahra gave, and looked at Alex. "Well?"

Alex glanced at her face then back to the wound and sighed. "I'd rather get moving too, and leave the ambulance for Amir and his buddies. Been a while since I stitched anyone up though."

"I'd do it, but if we're going to the hospital anyway, the staff there will just take everything out when they treat her, and they'll be able to do a better job of irrigating it than I can here." Gage tucked his sidearm into his shoulder holster as he came around the back. "Unless you want to stitch her up," he said to Sean, obviously not wanting to overstep his boundaries with Zahra.

While Sean could do sutures if he had to, he'd prefer to not have to repeatedly stab a needle into her flesh after all she'd already been through. And besides, he was so keyed up about almost losing her that his hands probably wouldn't be steady. "Nah, just bind it up for now. I'll keep her warm."

"I'll stand watch," Alex announced, and went around the side to pull out a rifle before positioning himself between the SUV and the edge of the woods where Ellis and Hunter had disappeared into.

Sean climbed in beside Zahra. He squeezed between her and the back of the seat to act as a bolster, wrapping his arms around her waist and turning her to face him so the back of her wounded leg was more easily accessible. Gage reappeared with the med kit and started pulling on some latex gloves. "Gotta get you warmed up so you don't shiver so much and make it harder for Gage to stop the bleeding."

She didn't respond other than to lean her cheek against him and close her eyes. "Does Alex know about the weapon?"

"Oh, I'm very much aware of it," Alex answered from beside the vehicle. "Evers and some of his federal pals are questioning Amir while he gets a nice blood transfusion to keep him alive."

"Where did you guys even come from?" Zahra asked.

"We were close to Hunter and Ellis, helping out with recon when Sean's call got cut off and we all had a bad feeling so we headed here just in case. Amir said the other cell members came back to pick up the weapon, and confirmed it's some sort of portable EMP device."

"The other shooters had a vehicle. They left it on an access road, can't be more than a mile from here," Sean said.

"Amazing what kind of toys Hassani has at his disposal over here," Alex muttered sarcastically.

"Why use it here though? To target me at my cabin? That seems like such a waste of effort, it doesn't make any sense," Zahra added, flinching as Gage probed at the wound. Sean hugged her tighter, wishing he could make the pain go away.

"It's a statement," Alex answered. "He's a goddamn self righteous megalomaniac and wanted us to know he has access to the technology, to show us what he's capable of unleashing here in the states on a broader scale. This is his way of giving us a taste of what's in store if we don't catch him in time to stop it. He thought he could use Amir's connection with your father to get to you, and through you to the rest of us."

"Just fucking with our heads," Gage agreed matter-of-factly, then glanced up at her questioningly. "This'll only take me a few minutes. You want me to freeze this first though?"

"If it'll take too long then I guess I can handle it without," she said hesitantly.

Sean huffed out a breath. "Freeze it," he said to Gage. Jesus, she didn't need to prove to the rest of them how tough she was and he had no desire to stand by and watch her suffer through more pain if relief was available.

Zahra tensed and sucked in a sharp breath when Gage injected the wound with lidocaine. "I know, stings like a motherfucker, doesn't it? Give it another minute and you won't feel anything at all. There's a small hospital less than an hour from here. I'll tape this all up for the trip."

"Yeah, fine. I just want this over with so we can get moving." She tipped her head up and looked at Sean. "Where are we going to stay?"

"After the hospital you're both coming to my place," Alex answered before Sean could say anything, and neither he nor Zahra argued. It was obvious Alex felt protective of Zahra and wanted to keep watch over her himself. Which was fine as long as he realized that Sean wasn't leaving her side.

Zahra closed her eyes again when Gage started binding up her leg. The edges of the wound were jagged due to the bullet's angle. Watching Gage pack and bind her leg, Sean was filled with anger at the shooter and himself all over again. He counted almost four minutes passing before Gage finished and reached for another syringe.

"Roll over," Gage said cheerfully.

Sean helped her ease onto her side and unzipped her jeans so she could wiggle them down far enough to expose her right hip. The sight of the surgical scars puckering her smooth skin there made Sean's throat burn. She'd been through so much, too much, and all he wanted to do was hide her away from the world so nothing could ever hurt her again.

Gage made quick work of injecting the antibiotics into her hip and peeled off his gloves. "I'll get you some pain pills and water in a sec." When he went back to the front of the SUV Sean slid out from behind Zahra and carefully eased her out into his arms. Carrying her to the back seat, he set her down and climbed in beside her. She accepted the pills and water from Gage and swallowed them down.

Gage nodded and stepped back, tapping his earpiece with a finger. "Go ahead… That's affirm… Roger that." He climbed in behind the wheel. "Boys are on their way out. One

KIA and one wounded, but he's unconscious and probably won't make it. K-9 unit already found the vehicle. Feds are having a field day drooling over the weapon."

"That's because it's one of our own top secret prototypes no one was supposed to have access to," Alex muttered as he strode around to the front passenger door. He slid in and shut the door. "Hunt and Ellis will catch a ride back with the Feds. Someone will stop by your place and grab your stuff, make sure nothing's been tampered with," he said to Zahra then spoke to Gage. "Let's get to that hospital."

So Zahra wouldn't have to see the body and the wounded shooter when their teammates brought them out. Sean sighed in relief and draped an arm around her shoulders. "Sleep if you want to," he said softly next to her ear as Gage started the engine and drove away.

She shook her head but snuggled up close as though she needed to feel him against her. Glad for the opportunity to hold her, Sean wrapped both arms around her and stared out his window into the darkness.

CHAPTER EIGHTEEN

It seemed like a short trip from the hospital back to the outskirts of Baltimore. Zahra's eyelids were drooping, lulled by Sean's body heat and the rhythmic purr of the engine. With eleven stitches, a tetanus booster and some codeine in her system she was good to go. The ER staff had debrided, irrigated and stitched the wound, verified there were no fractures, then gave her a prescription for pain meds. She was relieved to know she wouldn't need any further treatment. After being delayed another hour by interviews with both the police and the FBI agents Evers had sent to meet them at the hospital, she just wanted to crawl into bed.

She covered a yawn and sat up when Gage exited off the freeway and headed for Alex's place. She'd never been there before, not in all the time she'd known him, and she was surprised that he wanted her to stay there now. It filled her with warmth to know he cared so much about her and knew he was upset about what had happened to her these past few days.

But she was more worried about Sean's reaction to everything. He'd been silent since leaving the hospital and she could feel him pulling back from her mentally. She knew it was because he felt guilty and responsible for what happened, but that was fucking stupid. The man had held off two shooters in almost complete darkness to protect her, and had managed to hit both men from what she was willing to bet was a hell of a lot farther away than the shot she'd taken.

Having never fired a weapon before let alone at someone, she thought her conscience would be bothering her but it wasn't. In fact, she felt vindicated by her actions. Empowered, in a way. She knew Amir would have killed her if he'd had the chance tonight so pulling the trigger had been an act of self defense, pure and simple.

She sat up a little and reached for Sean's hand. He glanced down at her and she was relieved when he wrapped his fingers around hers and squeezed. Despite the pain meds her leg throbbed like a separate heart beat and all she wanted was to get to Alex's place so she could be alone with Sean. She needed to feel him against her, skin to skin.

Gage pulled into the driveway of a white two story Colonial style house in a quiet residential area with mature trees lining the street and dropped them off. Sean carried her inside and up to the guest room Alex showed them to. Poor man had fielded calls all the way back from the hospital and his cell rang again as he opened the bedroom door for Sean. From what she'd overheard, she was pretty sure this latest conversation was going to be about the mole.

Alex sighed and pulled out his phone. "You guys need anything, I'll be downstairs in my office."

"Thanks," she said, secretly glad that she and Sean would have even more privacy.

Sean shut the door behind them and carried her over to the queen size bed. He pulled back the covers and gently set her down on her side, using the extra pillows to prop up her leg and relieve pressure on the wound. "You need anything? Food? Want to ice your leg for a bit?"

"No, I just want to get out of these dirty clothes. Can you help me into a bath if I prop my leg over the side?"

"Sure."

She sat up slightly to peel the sweater up and over her head. "Help me with my jeans?" Undoing the button and zipper, she hooked her fingers in the waistband and eased them over her hips. Sean helped her drag them down over her legs, slowing to get the left one over the wad of bandages. The hospital had cut her jeans to make their job easier but it was still a tight fit. She flinched and he swore.

"Sorry."

"It's okay, just get it off." She couldn't wait to wash the scent of blood and the forest off her.

He tugged them off as gently as he could and tossed them aside, then helped her with her panties while she took off her bra. At the sight of her naked he swallowed and stood up. "I'll start the water. Hang tight." He disappeared into the connecting bathroom and started filling the tub. When he came back and scooped her up, she looped her arms around his neck for the ride into the bathroom. Gently settling her into the water, he piled a few towels up under her leg to cushion it from the edge of the tub, then stroked her hair back from her forehead. "Okay?"

She nodded, just wanting to be alone for a few minutes. "Thanks."

Seeming to understand that, he nodded and stood. "I'll be outside if you need me."

He closed the door behind him. Zahra closed her eyes and leaned her head back with a tired sigh. The hot water felt good, soothing her tight, sore muscles. She grabbed the soap and washcloth he'd set out for her and cleaned up as best she could. Sean must have heard her drain the tub because he came back in seconds later to wrap her in a towel. Touched by his attentiveness, she smiled into his shoulder when he carried her back to the bed, removed the damp towel from her body and covered her up.

Then he straightened and ran a hand through his hair, looking exhausted. "I need a quick shower."

"Go ahead, I'm fine." Just kind of numb and…empty.

He turned off the light on the nightstand and went back into the bathroom. The shower turned on. She envisioned Sean standing naked beneath the rush of hot water, fat rivulets of it running down his muscled body. She hugged her pillow tighter, aching to feel his arms around her, his body pressed flush against hers. Those terrifying moments in the forest tonight had torn her wide open, leaving her raw and emotional. Only Sean could heal her right now.

He emerged from the bathroom a few minutes later in a cloud of steam and flicked off the light before she'd gotten more than a glimpse of him wearing nothing but a towel around his lean waist. The image of all those muscles sent a wave of arousal through her. His footsteps were hushed against the carpet. "Still doing okay?" Her eyes adjusted to the soft outside light filtering through the blinds above the bed. He seemed hesitant, as if he didn't know what to do next.

Zahra snagged his hand and pulled. "Just lie down with me." Thankfully he didn't hesitate. He stretched out next to her on his side and she immediately reached for him, grabbing those wide, strong shoulders. She held on tight and buried her nose in the center of his chest, squeezing her eyes shut on a sigh when he wrapped his arms around her.

They laid that way for a few minutes, pressed close to one another in the darkness, the only sounds their breathing and the throb of his heart close to her ear. He felt like heaven, warm and strong around her. The hot, hard length of his erection pressed into her stomach. Her skin tingled all over, goose bumps skittering over her body as arousal ignited. Even though she was exhausted and in pain, she needed him to make love to her.

His hand stroked her back. "Cold?"

She shook her head. Not cold at all. She felt horny and needy and fragile all at once.

Letting her emotions guide her for once, she ran her hands down his muscular back to his ass and squeezed, bringing that rigid column of flesh harder against her. Sean swallowed audibly and hugged her tighter, thankfully didn't resist when she reached between them to wrap her fingers around him.

He made a low, tortured sound and grabbed her wrist. "Baby, you're sore and I don't want to hurt you."

"It hurts more without this." She trailed kisses across his chest, licked and nibbled at the tight beads of his nipples and earned a sharp intake of breath. Her fingers stroked his cock slowly, her core wet and ready for him. "I need you inside me." Needed it in a way she couldn't put into words.

Strong fingers wound into her hair. He tilted her head back and took her mouth in a scorching kiss. Moaning, Zahra grabbed the back of his head with one hand and thrust her tongue against his, moving her hips in tiny circles against his thigh to give her the friction she needed. She was already wet, the motion of her hips rubbing over the swollen bundle of nerves at the top of her sex. As good as it felt, she wanted the feel of him sliding into her, stretching and filling her, possessing her. She reached down and started to push him into her.

With a soft growl, Sean pulled back. "No condom."

"I'm clean," she panted against his mouth. "Are you?"

"Yeah." He caressed her tongue with his. "Still can't though."

She made a frustrated sound. "Just pull out later. Please, Sean, I *need* you inside me."

He sat up and got off the bed, leaving her feeling cold. Confused, bereft, she eased up on an elbow and opened her mouth to ask him what was wrong when she realized he was only coming around the other side of the bed. He slid in behind her this time, those beautiful hands roaming over her skin. Once she was arching into his touch he positioned her back on her side with a pillow propping her leg up and gently eased her thigh forward, opening her to him.

She moaned when he fitted himself behind her, molding her curves to his hardness. "Stay still for me," he ordered. "You let me do all the work or this doesn't happen."

All she could do was nod and pray he'd hurry up already. Her inner muscles squeezed in greedy anticipation of the moment he'd finally thrust into her. She reached back to wind a hand around the back of his neck. "Not too gentle though. I need to feel you take me." It was the best way she could explain what she needed.

He made a low, hungry sound that sent a flare of heat bolting into the pit of her stomach, and nipped the tender place where her neck and shoulder met. "Just don't move," he warned, soothing the little sting with his tongue.

Zahra closed her eyes and allowed her body to relax into his care. He captured a nipple between his thumb and forefinger and squeezed, rolling it as he circled his cock against her hips and lavished her neck and shoulders with hungry, open-mouth kisses. Humming in pleasure, she bit her lip when he skimmed a hand down her belly and between her thighs.

He groaned as his fingers stroked the swollen folds. "So damn wet, Zahra."

"Please," she whispered, her body so full of tension she wanted to scream.

His hot breath fanned against the back of her neck. "Gonna fuck you so deep now, baby."

Oh my God. "Please," she repeated in a desperate voice, fingers digging into his nape, spine arched taut as she waited for him to stop tormenting her.

The hand between her thighs eased back and a moment later she felt the hot, blunt head of his cock against her opening. She held her breath, trembling, dying for the moment when he drove inside. He rolled her nipple again and plunged deep with a single twist of his hips that dragged a shattered cry from her.

Sean released her nipple and covered her mouth with his palm to stifle the sound, breathing hard against her neck. "God, you're so fucking hot and perfect around me." His voice was hoarse, strained.

The feel of him buried so deep inside her, the incredible fullness and heat made her whimper. To be held and filled and loved by this man was the most shatteringly beautiful thing she'd ever experienced. Emotion swamped her, tearing past all resistance until tears flooded her eyes. She made a choked sound and strained back against him, hoping he realized the crying was cathartic and not because she was in pain.

Thankfully he seemed to understand. Keeping that hand cupped over her mouth he pulled back and eased forward, fucking her in a slow, deep rhythm as his fingers played between her legs. Pleasure jolted through her entire body, magnifying each time he slid over that sweet spot inside her. Her moans turned desperate, her core clamping down on him as the pressure built. The low, strained sounds he made only added to the heat, telling her how good it felt and how much he enjoyed being inside her. He was so hard, so hot, stroking every quivering nerve ending inside her.

The wave built higher, higher as he pumped and stroked and groaned against her neck. When it finally hit she sobbed and let go, her muscles cording up. A flare of pain shot up her wounded leg but she didn't care, the pleasure and emotional release eclipsing everything else. As she came back to earth she realized tears were rolling down her face. Sean had released her mouth to hold her tight, still buried deep inside her. He breathed roughly against the back of her neck, his muscles so tight she knew he must be in agony needing to come. Tightening her inner walls around him she circled her hips slightly.

His arm contracted around her waist and he sucked in a harsh breath. "Don't."

"Want to feel you come," she murmured. "Want you to mark me."

The answering growl he made sent a primal shiver through her. He nibbled at the side of her neck. "Say you're mine."

She smiled at his possessiveness and arched her neck. "I'm yours. Make me yours."

"All mine," he muttered, his arms locked tight around her and then he took her hard and fast. Zahra gasped and pressed back for more, loving the feeling of him letting go, of being claimed. Their damp skin slipped and slid together as he plunged in and out of her. His breathing sped up, tremors wracking his muscles as he took what he needed. At the last moment he gripped her hips hard and pulled out. With a deep, guttural groan he bit the top of her shoulder and came against her lower back in long hot spurts.

He sagged behind her, resting his head behind hers on the pillow. His hands resumed stroking over her naked skin, skimming the curves of her waist and hips. Soft kisses trailed over the top of her head. "I'll get a cloth."

Zahra hummed in response and didn't open her eyes. She heard the tap turn on in the bathroom sink, then his quiet footfalls returning. The bed dipped and he stroked her hair back from her face. She leaned her cheek into his hand then a warm, damp cloth touched her tearstained face. He washed away her tears gently before reaching around to clean her hips and lower back, then pulled the covers over her. Moments later he stretched out on his side facing her and ran a finger down the side of her face. She opened her eyes and smiled up at him in the dimness.

"How's your leg?"

"Better now, thanks." She felt like a contented kitten curled up for a nap in a puddle of sunlight.

He smiled back. "You never have to thank me for that. I do love it when you beg though. And when you get all demanding about me marking you. That was hot."

She laughed softly, loving the mischievous twinkle in his eyes. "I wanted it." Grasping his wrist to maintain the connection between them, she basked in the quiet intimacy while he ran gentle fingertips over her face. Her heart was so full for him. Though it scared her to death to expose herself in the face of possible rejection, she couldn't hold her feelings inside any longer. She'd come close to dying tonight and didn't want to spend another night on earth without him knowing what she felt.

"I'm falling in love with you."

Her eyes snapped open at his soft admission. She'd never expected him to say it at all, let alone admit it first. "I think I'm falling in love with you too."

His fingers stilled on her cheek, his eyes flaring. "You *think*? You're not sure?"

She swallowed, heart pounding. "Okay, I'm sure." Tell him the truth. "And I've already fallen."

Groaning, Sean kissed her, his big hand curling around the back of her head in a possessive move that melted her. "Then tell me," he whispered against her lips. "Say it right."

"I'm in love with you," she whispered back, sliding her hands into his hair.

"God, Zahra." He kissed her until she moaned and squirmed in his hold, then eased back with a wicked grin despite her whimper of protest. "No more of that kind of medicine tonight."

"In the morning then?"

"Hmm, we'll see." He trailed a hand down her spine to cup her bottom and squeeze. Propping his head in his hand, he stared down at her thoughtfully. "Alex will give us a few days together if we ask him. Come to Coeur d'Alene with me. I want you to meet my family."

A startled smile broke over her face. She hadn't expected him to ask something like that and it surprised and delighted her. "I'd like that."

"Good." He dropped another kiss on her mouth. "We'll see how you're feeling in the morning, but if you're up to it we can fly out tomorrow."

"Sounds good to me." She sighed in contentment when he laid back down and wrapped his arms around her. Snuggling in close to his warmth, she closed her eyes and smiled in the darkness.

The NSA contact didn't answer his call. It was the third attempt Malik had made in the past four hours.

The authorities must have figured out who the mole was, and arrested them. Which meant he no longer had anyone inside the NSA to help him with his plans. It also meant he'd just burned his own location by calling the damn encrypted phone number.

Curling his free hand into a fist, he slammed his phone onto his desk, fracturing the screen. His advisors had informed him of Amir's failure mere hours ago, and that he was currently dying in a Baltimore hospital. Malik's only comfort was knowing that the man would soon join his other fellow cell members in death. Both Abdullo and the former American army soldier known as Bob were currently in refrigerated drawers at a Baltimore morgue.

They'd failed to kill any of the Titanium members yet again and had let the weapon fall back into American hands. With all the evidence Amir was no doubt spewing forth as fast as his dying brain would allow, it was only a matter of time before the Americans realized where Malik was.

Shouting for his bodyguards, he tore open his office door and stalked through the house to the garage. The two men hurried ahead to make sure everything was secure and one opened the back door of his SUV for him. Malik climbed inside and settled himself into the plush leather seat. "Take me to the safe house in Peshawar," he ordered the bodyguard behind the wheel.

As the vehicle raced away from the house he'd never set foot in again, Malik stared out the window at the sun-baked landscape. The remaining men at the house he'd just left would take care of destroying and disposing of his computer and cell phone and as always his bug-out bag was packed and in the trunk right now. If the Americans hadn't yet evacuated them he'd still make good his threat about killing the mole's family. That lesson would serve as another example of what happened to the people who crossed him, and what could happen to those they loved.

He leaned his head against the headrest, planning for what must come next. Precautions, security measures and the next phase of his plans to unleash more attacks in the US. He wasn't a fool. He knew the Americans would be coming soon to hunt him on his home turf and he would be ready when they did. They'd soon learn he wasn't an easy man to target and that his many friends in high places would make their attempts at locating him a deadly effort.

CHAPTER NINETEEN

Alex set the phone receiver back into the cradle on his desk at NSA headquarters, braced his forearms on the cool wooden surface and let his head drop forward with a weary sigh.

Damn.

He closed his eyes for a moment. Part of him wanted to deny what he'd just been told, but he was too jaded to allow himself to entertain such blissful ignorance even for a second.

Evers and the other Feds working on the case had just confirmed the identity of the mole, beyond any shadow of a doubt. And now Alex felt sick to his stomach.

He'd suspected who it was a few days ago, then dismissed the idea as him being paranoid only to grow suspicious all over again. It was why he'd given Evers the go ahead to obtain the search warrant at the suspect's house yesterday morning. They'd found the encrypted throw away phone only hours ago. Analysts at Quantico had discovered the damning evidence: a series of phone calls received from a secret number in Pakistan.

They all knew who the caller was.

Somehow, with every anti-terrorism agency in the country and its American allies looking for him, Malik Hassani was still in fucking *Pakistan*. In fact, it looked like he'd been there all along, maybe even because of help from the ISI and certain high ranking officers in the Pak military and police.

But unfortunately Alex had another, more immediate crisis to deal with at the moment.

He ran a hand over his prickly face and pushed up from his desk, suddenly exhausted. After no sleep for the past forty-eight hours and last night's scary-ass incident with Zahra, he felt every one of his fifty-one years.

With a heavy heart he opened his door and strode down the hallway. People were busy at their desks and cubicles, business as usual on this typical Thursday morning.

But this was anything but business as usual.

He kept his gaze straight ahead, not glancing at the other employees he passed who smiled or said hello. Details tumbled through his mind, little things he couldn't believe he hadn't noticed before yesterday. The fatigue. The extreme anxiety during the interview he'd dismissed as a normal response to an unfamiliar and intimidating situation. Working extremely late hours, then being the first to arrive in the morning even though some of the team members were back in the conference room mere hours after going home to snatch a little sleep.

He now saw that what he'd previously viewed as dedication for what it had truly been.

Opportunities to sneak information from his office and report back to Hassani.

Understanding the why of it might make him sympathetic, but it didn't change facts. He had no other choice than to turn the mole over to the Feds, no matter how much he wished it had turned out differently.

Anger and betrayal warred in his heart as he passed the last office and headed for the desk near the elevator bank. His footsteps were almost silent on the carpet. She didn't hear him coming. Her back was to him, her silver head bent slightly as she typed something at her keyboard. Alex stopped beside her desk, noting the framed pictures of her daughter, son-in-law and grandkids. The collateral Hassani had wielded over his longest, most loyal employee.

Ruth stopped typing. Her shoulders went rigid. When she finally risked a glance up at him he caught the raw fear in her gaze and his gut twisted.

She knew he knew.

Ah, shit, what a goddamn mess. He'd do what he could to protect her, though it wouldn't be enough to save her from a prison sentence for treason.

Placing his hands on her desk, he leaned down and stared directly into those frightened eyes. He would have preferred to have this conversation in the privacy of his office but here was good enough. "Is there something you need to tell me, Ruth?" he asked quietly.

Tears instantly flooded her eyes. Her expression crumpled and she put her hands to her face. "I'm sorry," she whispered shakily as tears flashed down her face, her eyes begging forgiveness. "I didn't want to hurt anyone, but I didn't have a choice. He said if I came to you or told anyone he would kill them. All of them, even my babies. He sent me pictures of them at school in their little uniforms, told me he had people there posing as guards who would kidnap and kill them with one word from him. I had to do what he said. I c-couldn't let him hurt my babies…" She covered her face in her hands and dissolved into wracking sobs.

Cursing silently, Alex rounded the desk, knelt and tugged her into his arms. "I know." He realized she'd felt she had no choice and that her actions were guided by the driving need to protect her family. "You know I wouldn't have let him hurt them, Ruth. You should've come to me, I could have made this stop weeks ago." That only made her cry harder.

"I was too scared he'd d-do it. I c-couldn't risk it."

He sighed. "A team of undercover FBI agents has already gone in to evacuate your son and his family, okay? They're all being moved out of Jordan as we speak and will arrive on a plane tonight at Dulles."

"Oh, th-thank you. Oh God, *thank* you." She shuddered then slumped in his arms, her relief palpable.

"You're welcome," he said quietly. Unfortunately it was the only comfort he could give her at the moment, because she was in a shitload of trouble and the severity of the consequences would depend on how fully she cooperated with the authorities involved. Alex just hoped it wasn't too late to undo the damage she'd caused to the investigation to capture Hassani.

Zahra was starving. Since Claire had just gone upstairs to put on a load of laundry, Zahra limped into Gage and Claire's kitchen from the living room in their temporary safe house. She and Sean had driven over at lunch time to meet up with everybody, and even Tom Webster, the forty-something owner of Titanium Security, was there. All the guys were seated around the kitchen island and glanced up when Zahra entered.

Gage immediately stood to offer her his seat and she got her first view of why they were all gathered around the island like a testosterone laden pack of hungry wolves. They had food in here, dammit, and they were hoarding it all.

Scowling, she hobbled over and sat on the stool Gage had vacated for her. "Were you guys going to share?"

"I was gonna bring you a plate," Sean swore, stuffing the last of a brownie he'd demolished into his mouth. A crumb-filled plate sat before him, only two brownies left. The sight of them sent a pang of sadness through her because they made her think of Ruth. Zahra hadn't known her well but her betrayal still stung. When Ruth had told Hassani that Zahra was attending the awards dinner, she'd effectively made her a sitting target.

And yet, despite all that, Zahra couldn't deny the thread of empathy she felt for the woman. A tiny thread, but still. Ruth had been in a truly terrible predicament and even now had to be scared to death that Hassani would take his revenge and kill her family members. Zahra still wanted her punished for what she'd done though.

Pushing the depressing thoughts away, she narrowed her eyes at Sean and reached for a potato skin from the platter in front of Hunter. "I'd like to believe that." *Especially since I just confessed that I'm in love with you*, she added with her eyes.

His eyes widened in feigned hurt. "I totally was!"

"Who made all this, anyway?"

"Gage," Hunter answered, stuffing his face with baked mushroom caps. "He's a regular Martha Stewart."

She eyed the redheaded second-in-command. "You bake too?"

He shrugged. "I'm just full of surprises, aren't I?"

Yeah, he was.

"How're those stitches holding up?"

"Good. The doctor said I can have them out in a week or so." Her leg hurt like freaking hell though. Way too sore to even contemplate sex when the pain had woken her just after dawn. Alex had been gone long before Sean helped her out of bed and he'd called less than two hours ago to tell her about Ruth.

It was so hard to wrap her head around that and it made her even more anxious to get to Coeur d'Alene and decompress for a few days. Gunshot wound or not, she wasn't going to let that stop her from getting on a plane this afternoon with Sean.

Since she was starving, she happily munched on the finger foods assembled before her while the guys got back to their conversation.

Tom swallowed a sip of his beer and rested a forearm against the edge of the granite topped island. "If we get the word to go wheels up for Pakistan, I've got a problem."

At the mention of Pakistan her appetite took a serious nose dive but she swallowed her mouthful anyway and kept listening. Some part of her had known that Sean would probably be sent there once they got a lock on Hassani, but she hadn't expected it to happen yet.

"With all the other jobs the company's got going on, I'm stretched thin for manpower. I've got those two guys you mentioned lined up for interviews in two days, Hunt. What about the rest of you? Got any recommendations for someone I might want to hit up for a job? Ideally someone that's as good with machines as they are with a long gun?"

At that, Sean stopped chewing what was no doubt his gazillionth brownie. Ellis glanced up from his plate of jalapeno poppers. They looked at each other, engaged in some sort of silent exchange, then Sean raised an eyebrow at the other man.

Tom took another pull of his beer, watching the two of them. "Ellis? You got someone in mind?"

The quiet sniper looked away from Sean and met his boss's gaze. "Maybe."

"They're a mechanic and a good shot?"

"Yeah."

"I know I probably don't have to ask this, but former military?"

"Marine."

Tom set his bottle down, seeming very pleased by this turn of events. "Can you ask them if they're interested?"

Ellis seemed to hesitate a moment before conceding with a nod. "I can try. Their shop is a few hours away. I could go by there in person tomorrow."

"Like to be a fly on the wall for that conversation," Sean muttered, and grabbed the second to last brownie.

Ellis shot him a censoring look, then glanced at the brownie and seemed to hold back a grin as he responded. "You wish."

Since apparently neither of them were going to divulge more than that, Zahra made a mental note to grill Sean about it on the flight and reached for the last brownie before he could snag it.

Gage stepped in front of her just as she stretched her arm out, blocking her. Looking up at him, she met his eyes and caught the nearly imperceptible shake of his head before he stepped away, carrying a plate to the sink. Frowning, she glanced at Hunter, who added a pointed look at the brownie and a tiny head shake of his own.

Confused and dying for a taste of that fudgy brownie, she suddenly realized that all the men were staring at Sean as he chewed on the brownie in his hand. He seemed to notice this at the same moment as her, and stopped chewing. "What?" he demanded, glancing around the table. "I left one."

"Oh, no, it's all yours," Hunter said in a sardonic tone and all the others snickered.

Zahra locked eyes with Sean. What the hell had they done to the brownies?

She watched the suspicion transform Sean's features. He slowly swallowed his mouthful and set the last bit of brownie in his fingers back onto his plate, a little pale all of a sudden. "What the fuck did you do?" he demanded of Hunter, scowling.

"Not a thing," Hunter answered, smiling as he polished off another tidbit from his own plate. Zahra noticed that not a single one of the plates in front of the guys had brownie crumbs except for Sean's.

Oh, no...

Sean whirled on Gage. "What did you do?" He stood up and wiped at his mouth as though he could scrub away and erase what he'd eaten.

Gage shrugged, his blue eyes dancing with glee. "Secret ingredient brownies. Hunt added the secret ingredient though."

Sean rounded on the team leader. "What the hell's in them, man?"

Snickering, Hunter stood and picked up his plate. "Chocolate. Mostly made up of extra strength laxatives."

Zahra covered her mouth with a hand as the other guys broke into howls of laughter.

"You asshole," Sean snarled, then stared in horror at the lone brownie on the platter. "*Shit.*"

"Yep, that about covers it, on both counts. Payback's a bitch, ain't it? You guys have a good flight this afternoon." Hunter winked at Zahra and took his plate to the sink as well.

Pale, a little sweaty, Sean put a hand to his stomach and looked up at her. "Oh my God, I ate six of them."

Wonderful, she thought with a grudging giggle, knowing she'd never understand what made these alpha males tick. Wasn't this going to be a fun trip to Coeur d'Alene?

EPILOGUE

Seated on Sean's mother's favorite chair in the living room with her leg propped up on an ottoman and a cozy flannel throw tucked around her, Zahra soaked up the comfort of the house Sean had grown up in. Just the immediate family was there because Sean's sister-in-law and niece were away visiting her parents in Washington State. Mrs. Dunphy was currently in the kitchen putting the finishing touches on dinner while Sean was outside with his dad and brother manning the grill. While she felt dumb sitting on her ass during her first impression with the family, no one would let her lift a finger, much less get up to help any of them. The flight had left her leg and even her foot swollen, so the rest felt wonderful.

The afternoon and plane ride had been eventful, since Sean had made frequent use of the facilities despite the bottle of anti-diarrhea medication he'd gobbled down in a futile effort to combat the laxative-laced brownies. As soon as he'd found out what Hunter and Gage had done, Sean did what any sane person would and ran to the bathroom to jam his finger down his throat and puke up everything he could.

She didn't know how much of the stuff Hunter and Gage had put into the batter, but it must have been a lot because even with the little bit that Sean had actually ingested, he couldn't make it more than half an hour without bolting for the bathroom. It would have been funnier than hell if she hadn't felt so bad for the guy. Not that this lesson would do anything to stop him from pulling more pranks on the others in the future. No, she was pretty sure this had only sparked a prank war.

Sean's mother came out of the kitchen with a glass of iced tea and a small plate of sliced homemade banana bread. She was a friendly, petite woman with dark brown hair styled into a sleek angled bob, and dark eyes that crinkled around the corners when she smiled. She set them down on the side table next to Zahra just as Sean came in from the deck through the sliding glass doors. Without glancing at them he rushed up the stairs for the guest bathroom once more.

His mother shook her head and grinned as she sank onto the sofa next to Zahra's chair. "First time that boy brings home a woman he's serious about and he's so nervous he's in the bathroom all night."

Zahra smothered a laugh, deciding not to reveal the true source of Sean's torment. "I'm really the first?"

The woman's deep brown eyes sparkled with warmth. "You are. So I'm doubly thrilled that you've come to visit. We don't get to see Sean as often as we'd like, with his job and all the traveling he has to do. Maybe now he'll come home more often and bring you with him."

While everything was new and she didn't know exactly what sort of expectations she had for their relationship, Zahra did know she wanted to be a permanent part of his life. "I'd like that." She picked up her glass of iced tea to give her hands something to do so she wouldn't fidget. Being here was the perfect break for her, but seeing the tight knit family dynamic going on put a lump in her throat. She'd never been part of a real family before and right now missed her mom more than ever.

"Do you need anything else? Dinner won't be much longer."

"No, this is perfect, thanks." It felt strange to have strangers fussing over her, but kind of nice.

Sean emerged at the foot of the stairs a few moments later, still looking a little pale. His mother shook her head at him. "There's really no need to be so nervous," she chided. "We've already decided she's a keeper."

A proud smile broke over his face as he crossed the room toward them. "I already decided that too."

His mom flashed her a wide-eyed *Oh-my-God-did-you-just-hear-that* look and did a terrible job of hiding her smile as she bit into a piece of banana bread. "So, how long did you say you'll be in town?" she asked him casually, though even Zahra could tell the question was anything but.

"A few days." Sean lowered himself onto the ottoman and carefully lifted her leg to position it across his thighs then took her foot between his strong hands, massaging her tender sole as he continued. Zahra barely held back a moan of bliss. "With the investigation taking off we'll both be needed back at work shortly. Luckily Zahra's boss has a soft spot for her and was willing to let me have some time off so I could whisk her away for a while."

"Well I should think so, after what happened to her," his mother replied indignantly, nodding at Zahra's bandaged leg. "But are you sure you don't want to stay here with us rather than at the hotel? Look at how comfy she is now. After dinner you can just tuck her in upstairs instead of putting her in the car and making her move around more than necessary getting around the hotel."

"Thanks, but we've already booked a room."

"So cancel it. For heaven's sake, if you're worried about needing to use the bathroom so much, just use the one downstairs later."

"It's not that." Sean looked up at Zahra and gave her a private smile. The heated look in his eyes, combined with the sinfully wonderful massage he was performing, made her toes curl and her belly flutter with anticipation. That look in his eyes told her that him wanting the privacy of a hotel room had nothing to do with his current predicament and everything to do with getting her naked and making her cry out his name once they were in bed.

His mother turned to her. "Zahra, it should be your call, so if you decide you want to stay here instead, you're more than welcome. Don't you let my son boss you around."

Zahra had to laugh. "Oh, you don't have to worry about that. He'll always know where he stands with me."

"Steaks are done," Sean's brother suddenly called through from out on the deck. "Let's eat, people."

Sean's mother shot her an encouraging smile and got up to head into the kitchen. Sean reached out to take Zahra's glass from her and eased out from beneath her sore leg. He knelt beside her chair and set a hand on the back of her neck. "We haven't even been here two hours and my mom's already in love with you. You are so in," he said with a laugh, leaning in to kiss her.

Seeing him so relaxed and happy, knowing that his family seemed to have accepted her so far, filled her with joy. "I like them. I've always wanted to be part of a real family," she added softly, feeling suddenly shy.

At her quiet admission he pulled back and searched her eyes. The answering tenderness in his gaze turned her heart over because she knew he understood what she meant. "Well hell, and you got stuck with mine?" Kissing her on the mouth once more, he pulled the blanket off her and lifted her into his arms. "Come on then, sweetness. Time to baptize you into the clan with your first official Dunphy dinner. Should be a memorable experience for you," he added wryly.

That it would be, and she was looking forward to it.

Wrapping her arms around his sturdy neck, Zahra snuggled into his strong embrace and allowed him to carry her to the dinner table where her new adoptive family waited.

—The End—

Complete Booklist

Titanium Security Series
(romantic suspense)

Ignited

Singed

Burned

Bagram Special Ops Series
(military romantic suspense)

Deadly Descent

Tactical Strike

Lethal Pursuit (September 2013)

Suspense Series
(romantic suspense)

Out of Her League

Cover of Darkness

No Turning Back

Relentless

Absolution

Empowered Series
(paranormal romance)

Darkest Caress

Historical Romance

The Vacant Chair

Acknowledgements

Another big thank you to my support team, Katie Reus and my hubby Todd. Your constant encouragement means so much to me and I appreciate the gift of you both being in my life! Love you guys.

Also, thanks to author Julieanne Reeves and J.R.T. editing, for giving this story a run through with fresh eyes. It needed it!

About the Author

Kaylea Cross writes edge-of-your-seat military romantic suspense. Her work has won many awards and has been nominated for both the Daphne du Maurier and the National Readers' Choice Awards. A Registered Massage Therapist by trade, Kaylea is also an avid gardener, artist, Civil War buff, Special Ops aficionado, belly dance enthusiast and former nationally-carded softball pitcher. She lives in Vancouver, BC with her husband and sons. You can visit Kaylea at www.kayleacross.com.

Made in the USA
Lexington, KY
01 March 2016